D0853670

The Living

Also by Anjali Joseph

Saraswati Park

Another Country

The Living

Anjali Joseph

FOURTH ESTATE • *London*

Fourth Estate
An imprint of HarperCollins Publishers
1 London Bridge Street
London SE1 9GF
www.4thEstate.co.uk

First published in Great Britain by Fourth Estate in 2016

1 3 5 7 9 8 6 4 2

An extract from this novel was previously published in *Granta 130: India*

A catalogue record for this book is available from the British Library

Hardback ISBN 978-0-00-746281-0
Trade paperback ISBN 978-0-00-746283-4

Typeset in Garamond

Printed and bound in Great Britain by Clays Ltd, St Ives plc

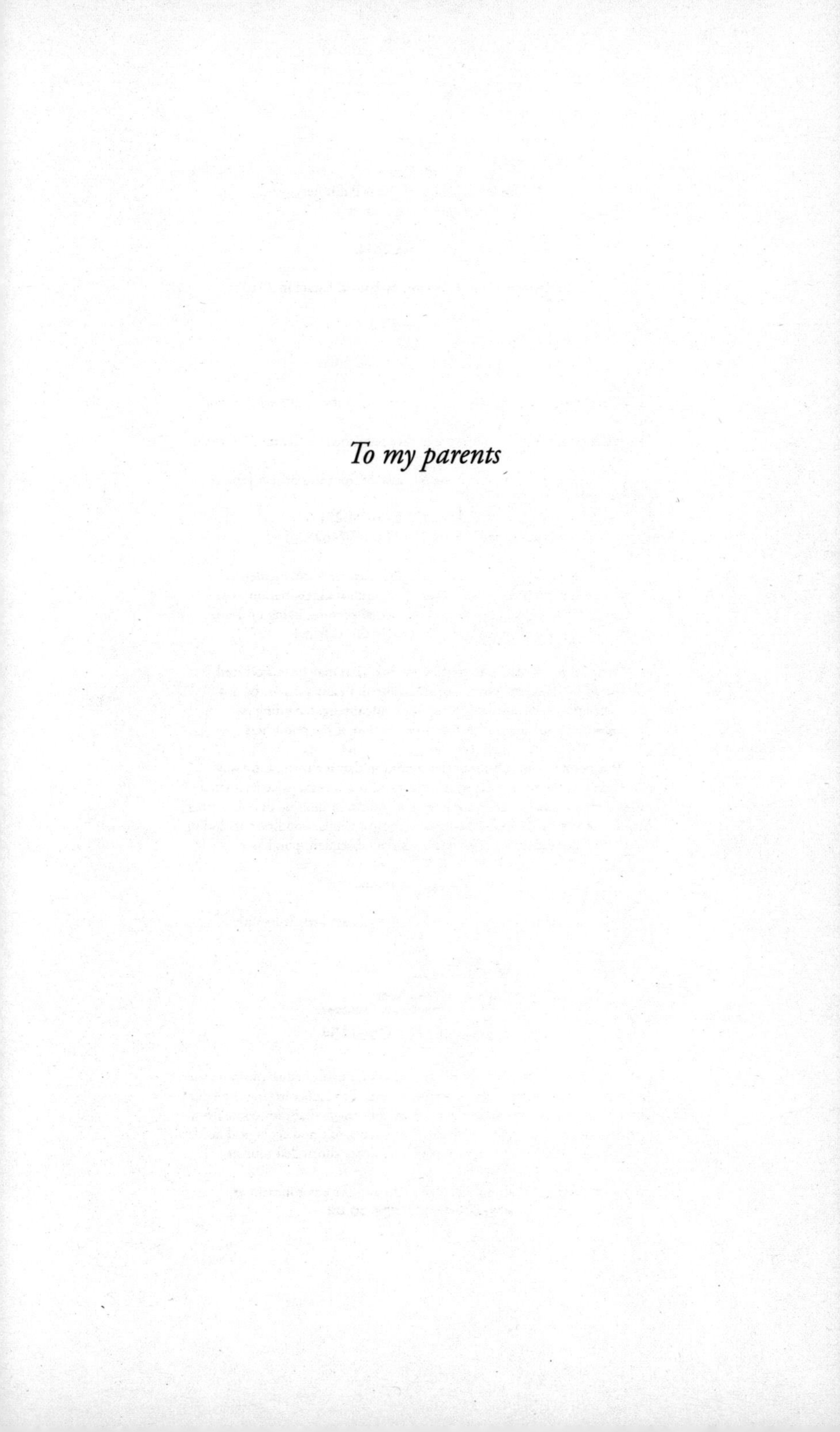

To my parents

The wise grieve neither for the living nor for the dead.

Bhagavad Gita, 2.11,
translated by Swami Sivananda

I

Shoes

1

A long way from the morning

This morning I couldn't open my eyes. It was light, mind you. Sunrise is that early now. But I wasn't waking up. The alarm went at a quarter to six so I could have tea, roll a fag, look at the sky, put on the radio quiet, take a shower. I left cereal on the table for Jason, and some fruit. It'd be there when I got home. Getting back at five … It's hard to imagine, like a place at the end of a walk, across fields, a river, a bridge, a forest, hills, and a motorway. It's a long way from the morning till the end of the day, a long long stretch.

Late. I flew down Plumstead Road, and up the inside way. My hair was wet, I was breathing too fast. By the time I came up the hill, the cathedral spire behind me, turned in at the factory shop and hurried through the gate it was a minute off seven thirty.

The morning had got brighter, real daylight. I came through the first door, and the second, up the little slope, through the double doors, hurried to my table, put away my bag and sat looking calm, trying not to breathe hard as the first bell went. From the corner of my eye I saw Jane's head move. She was stood talking to John near the heel attacher but her hair swung as she turned towards me. I put my head down and started checking the first box of Audrey, a vintage sling-back with a bow on the vamp. I got out my black wax stick and fixed a scuff on the toe. The roughing machine was on now and that first smell of leather was in the air, sweaty and sweet and sharp from the spray the men use in the lasting machines. The windows at the closing end were bright but high up and far away. The lights were on, they're always on, and it was warm, like it always is, from the machines, and there was the sound of the machines, the humming. I carried on checking the shoes, making sure they paired, and writing down how many times I'd done it and I heard the radio and other people's voices and felt everyone around me at their machines or their station and Jane moving about to check on things and that busyness there always is as the shoes move around all of us a busyness where each one is doing the same thing over and over but fast enjoying being able to do it smoothly but thinking too or in another place and it was like I'd always been there, never left, never gone home or done anything else, and that's how it always is.

2

Like heavy water

Mum, Jason was saying. I pulled myself out of a dream. I was on the sofa. What time is it? I said. It was eight thirty. The telly was on.

I've turned into one of those people who fall asleep on the sofa, I said. At thirty-five. All I wanted to do was go back into the dream, one of those tired ones where you're always on the move looking for something just around the next corner.

I was saying, Gran phoned today, Jason said.

Oh God, I said. I rubbed my face. When?

Before you got home.

Of course she did. No flies on her.

Mum, he said. Don't start. He was frowning.

I'm not starting, I said. Definitely not. I chewed on my bottom lip. What did she say? I asked.

She wants me to go round and see them. She said Granddad's not been well.

What did she say it is? I asked. Jason's face was in between, talking to me, but vulnerable too. She knows how to make him feel guilty.

He leaned against the doorway, dug a hand in his pocket. She said he's short of breath, he said, gets tired all the time. He watched, waiting to see if I was going to be unreasonable. I felt the nap of the sofa under my hand, fucked old velvet, and thought of the dream again, inescapable, like heavy water.

Okay, right, I said. How much was she making up, I wondered. I started looking around for my tobacco. Did she say he'd seen the doctor? I asked.

She said he says he's fine, but she's worried. They're getting older, he said.

Yeah, I said. I sometimes regret letting those people near him. Especially her. The way she behaved when I was pregnant. I licked the gum strip and stared at the end of my cigarette.

Here. Jason lit it for me. Mum, he said. Don't get into all that again, all that stuff from the past. His eyes held mine, blue and steady.

Okay, I said. I smoked, and felt depressed.

He straightened up. Anyway, he said, I told you. He squeezed my shoulder and went out.

You did, I said. I got up. Better do the washing-up, I said to no one. I did it carelessly and felt like the clattering dishes were harassing me. Afterwards I wiped up and cleaned the counters. I made my sandwiches. I had a shower and went to bed, but knew I wouldn't fall asleep for a while. My neck ached, and my shoulders. And I knew it'd be there, waiting to swallow me up: the humming of the machines, the smell of the aerosol, the leather dust, the lights, the heat. I wouldn't think about it when I'd got going and all day I'd be on the shop floor but something would be leaving me and at the end of the day I wouldn't even remember what it was.

3

Nothing's new

I thought I'd forgotten the phone call but it came back. I thought about it on the way to work, then decided I wouldn't think about it any more. Mum in her flowered apron in the kitchen making tea, her eyebrows raised, saying something, complaining. No one ever does things right. I'll have to tell him, she says. Why do you have to? Dad says.

I don't even know what they look like now. I've seen them since I left, now and again. They used to come and take Jason out for the afternoon. Before Christmas they'd come round with his present, and something for me. A scarf, a bath set. The presents made me angry. Everything about them makes me angry. Dad because he doesn't say anything, he just lets her go on. And her because …

I got to work on time and smiled at Tom. He's one of my favourite people. He's in his late sixties, over retirement age, but he keeps coming in. He likes it. He says he doesn't want to stay home, find ways to fill the time. He told me about his wife's grandparents once. They used to be the loveliest couple, but when he retired things changed. They started bickering. You'd look at them and think, That's not you. And about the retired men where he lives. He doesn't live this way, he's the other side of town. There's a man who goes out for his paper the same time every day, he says. An Indian gentleman, Mr Singh. You could set your watch by him. Every day he goes for a walk, but so slowly, because he's got nothing to hurry for. I'd hate to be like that.

All right, lass? Tom said. You look better today. He smiled.

I grinned at him. Better than what?

He looked down. All the while, his hand was working, pulling tight a last with the pincers. You were a bit at sixes and sevens, like, yesterday, he said.

And today? I said. Fives and tens?

He smiled, and hammered down the last with the end of the pincers. I like the way he still looks like a boy, small, his head neat.

I worked without thinking till it was near first break. There's a watchfulness about us all, like animals that measure time. When it gets near break we stop chatting or passing the time and finish as fast as we can. Then when the bell goes it's silent. People walking across the floor to the coffee machine, or a few of the men – John, Tom, Derek – sitting down near it. I took my coffee to sit with Helen in the closing section.

I like the older ladies. Jane was talking to Cathy near her machine. Cathy had the paper open. Karen was doing her puzzle, head down. You could hear the silence and people's heads humming. I had my book but I didn't read. I stared at the same part of the same page and thought about the spring when I'd moved into Nan's house, and all the things my mother said before I left. Don't think about it, Nan said. She's always been like that. My mother's face, her mouth drawn tight then opening to spit out something poisonous. Don't think about it, I thought. I thought about it furiously.

When the first bell went I shook myself and went to the loo. Someone had used the cubicle before me. I sat breathing in her smell. I thought, nothing's new. I washed my hands, didn't look in the mirror, and reached my station before the second bell went. The morning just passed.

4

A person who could be looked at

Jason's football practice today. I found myself slowing down on the way home. I went into the Three Bells. I sat in the garden with my shandy, thinking, there's nothing to do, nothing to do. It was bright, white clouds moving fast across the sky. It wasn't really warm, but it felt good to sit with my face in the sun. I drank slowly, and thought about smoking. A wasp buzzed around my glass. On another table there was a man with a lanky dog, maybe a lurcher. The man was drinking a pint and talking on the phone. The dog lay at his feet. Every now and then it got up and he would tear off a bit from a slim packet, probably a Peperami, and feed it.

After a while a couple came in. They sat down but got up again and went inside. Then a man on his own. I caught him looking, a sharp glance. Suddenly I thought about my clothes. I go to work wearing anything: jeans, a t-shirt. It's not worth wearing nice stuff, and anyway half the year I get dressed in the dark. Jane dresses up, but she isn't working like we are. She wears heels – not stilettos but two or three inches.

I looked at the man again, and saw him looking at me. Was he good-looking? I looked away. The wasp was getting in my drink. I waved my hand at it, caught the glass, and shandy slopped over the side.

Fuck, I said. I moved the glass and shifted away from the wet part of the bench. The man was smiling at me. He was blond, tall maybe, thinnish. His clothes fit well. He looked comfortable on his own, like he always looked the same. I found a tissue in my pocket and wiped shandy off my elbow. Yeah, very cool.

I stared under my hair at the glass, drank from it. I tried to imagine the way he might see me. He probably thought I fancied him. I didn't want to be looked at, I wasn't ready. Make a bit more effort, I thought. Try. Wear mascara. Do something with your hair. You're not dead yet. Something Nan used to say. I'm not dead yet. Then she'd smile. Had I forgotten how to live? Just going on, getting things done.

I finished the shandy, imagined myself outside the factory, and the same person inside, saw myself as though I wasn't me. A figure in the fluorescent light on the shop floor, walking there in the morning, leaving in the afternoon. A person who could be looked at without disappearing.

I pushed away the glass. A shadow went over me. It was the same man leaving. He slowed as he passed, and looked into my face. He smiled. Afternoon, he said. Nice day. I stared at him, like someone in a dark room when the light goes on. In the puddle of spilt shandy the wasp was on its side, buzzing and flailing. I had the urge to bring the glass down on it, then I was ashamed. I should have said something back. When I got up, I picked up the wasp on the edge of a beer mat and left it to dry in the sun. All the way home I was aware of myself, and my sticky elbow. What each person I passed near the shops and on the road saw when they looked at me, if they did look. I got home and took out the clothes I'd wear tomorrow.

5

Life was simple

By now I should know not to listen to Katie. I should know not to listen to you, I heard myself tell her at some point in the evening but by then we were both drunk. By now, I said. We thought it was funny. It was her round and she'd come back from the bar with two drinks and two shots of something green.

What the fuck do you think that is? I said. I'm not drinking that.

It's herbal, she said. She grinned. Come on, you can't be boring all your life.

I picked up the glass and tilted it about. Does it get the toilet whiter than it's ever been? I asked.

Wait and see, she said. She knocked hers back. I did the same. My throat burned and my eyes watered. Jesus, I said. She took it as a compliment.

Thursday night, she said. It's the best time.

I work on Fridays, I said.

Half day, she said, which was true.

Why can't we just go out on a Friday, or at the weekend? I said.

I'll tell you everything when I see you, she said.

She always wants to go somewhere different, whichever is the new best place. You wouldn't think there'd be so many, but she always knows – from someone at work, or someone she's met out. This time we were in a vodka bar off Tombland.

This place is all right, I said. It was black inside, with chrome railings, and high seats at tall tables. At the bar there were groups of girls ordering pitchers of cocktails. The music was loud.

She nodded. I do salsa here on Tuesdays, she said.

Salsa? You do salsa now?

I'm going to start zumba, she said. You should try it. It's a real laugh. She eyed me. You need to do new stuff, Claire. Shake things up. It's like life's –

It's like life's what?

She stirred her mojito and looked at me. Oh, just a sec Claire, she said. She checked her phone and started replying to a text. I watched her strong, toned arms, and the way she sat.

She put down the phone. What was I saying? she asked. Her eyes were vague.

It's like life – I said.

She focused on me. It's good to shake things up, Claire, she said. Change things.

Oh yeah, I said. You know me. Change, I love it.

I'd made an effort. I was wearing a dress, boots, eyeliner. I'd done my hair. I still felt invisible. The way she held herself, and her clothes, it was like she expected attention. And she got it. We were at a table near the door and all the men who passed looked at us quickly, a rush of cold air as the door opened, and then back at her as it closed.

She's always been this way. Not just with men, but always changing, on the move, rushing from one thing to another. She talked fast, ate fast, gulped her words down. Never had to wear a coat because she ran everywhere. That Katie's a hasty one, Nan used to say. Is she on her way to the moon?

So what's your news? I asked.

She'd met a man, at the accountancy firm. Maybe that's when she changed, I was thinking as she talked, after she did that course, and got her job in reception. New clothes, work, men. This one's name is Graham.

He's older, she said. He has his own house. Near Angel Road. He's got a son, Sean, he's seventeen. Graham's divorced. He's nice, she said. He takes me out for dinner, or we go bowling. It's nice to actually do stuff. For someone to make an effort, you know?

It sounds great, I said. I felt sad, as though things were leaving me behind. Oh, I like your hair, by the way, I said. It suits you.

Thanks! I think I might go blonde again, though, soon. She shook it out, dark brown strands. The last time I saw her it was red. When we were young her hair was light brown, mousy Nan called it. Katie started dyeing it when we were fourteen or fifteen.

Do you fancy going for a bit of a dance? she asked.

Maybe in a bit. Hey, I said, Jason said Mum called.

Oh, really? she said. Hang on, just a minute. Sorry, Claire. She stopped to check her phone. Graham wants to go away for the weekend, she said. Up to the coast.

That's nice, I said. I wish Mum would leave me alone.

Katie made a face. Maybe it's time to put water under the bridge, Claire, do you think? It's been a while.

Seventeen years, I said.

Katie changed. Her mouth became tight and angry, and her voice went nagging. Well, you always had to be special, didn't you, she said. You think you're better than other people.

Jesus, I said, don't.

She shrugged. Well, she said. You had your Nan. I ran into your mum the other day, by the way.

What? You didn't tell me. When?

Um, I can't remember. It was near Anglia Square. I was walking through on my way to Graham's. Evening time. She said hello to me, Hello Katie. I said hello, how are you, and all that stuff.

How did she look?

Kind of the same, a bit smaller, her hair was whiter. I see

her now and again, I bump into her. Once a year, something like that. It's not a big place, is it?

No, I said. I'm always surprised I don't run into them more. Maybe it's meant to be.

Katie rolled her eyes. Claire, she said. She leaned forward on her elbows. Why don't you do something different? Leave that job. Do something new.

Like what? I don't have any experience.

You could train. You could get some.

Doing what?

It'd be better paid.

This is a good job, I said. I mean, it's solid.

She shook her head. Then she told me more about Graham, and Sean. Sean was getting to like her, she said. He lived with his mum, but Graham was hoping when Sean went to university he'd spend more of the holidays with Graham and Katie.

When we said goodnight I was properly drunk. On the way home off the main road I found myself running, only because I could. I was light, and fast. The drink. I went to bed too late and in the morning everything hurt: my head, my arms and legs. It was only a half-day. I couldn't think because I was so tired. I kept drinking water, and felt a bit sick, but nothing happened. In a way I liked it, not being able to think. There was a sweetness to being hungover. Life was simple.

6

The day and what it wanted

I woke up aching, with a sore throat. My back hurt. That doesn't normally happen. I was having a dream. Brad Pitt came to start at the factory. I had to show him around. We ended up in bed. But people kept breaking into the room to talk to him. They wouldn't behave normally. Brad and I sat in bed discussing it, how people couldn't just be normal, couldn't be human. I got up thinking, Who'd have thought Brad would be so sensible? And, it's a pity it wasn't Johnny. And, my back hurts. My legs hurt. My shoulders hurt. I went to bed at eleven, lights out at midnight. Friday: you know you can do what you want, assuming you can remember what that is.

I made coffee, and sat on the sofa. Then lay down. My head was full of the people I knew, little aches, like insects buzzing. Katie, Helen, Sandra, who's Jason's friend Steve's mum, my older brother, haven't seen him for years, Dad. I didn't want to see any of them, but feeling them there made me more lonely. It was amazing how tired I was. I lay on my front and closed my eyes. I tried to ask myself what could be wrong. What should I do today? What's wrong? Go into town. Look at some shops. Have a coffee. Behave like a person. I couldn't even imagine the noise and press in the city on a Saturday coming up to summer. I didn't feel sick in an obvious way. Should I have a cigarette? I asked the quiet part of me, right inside. Should I have a cigarette? It said it really didn't matter, and that put me off more than the voice in my head saying, stop smoking, which always made me want to.

Mum, Jason said. He came in talking loudly. I can't find my shirt. My strip. I can't find it.

He wasn't upset yet. He was just raising the issue.

I said still face down, Have you looked in the laundry basket the airing cupboard under your bed your chest of drawers your kit bag?

I've looked everywhere, he said. He went to look in the places I'd said or some of them. The conversation would be continued. He came back in. Are you ill? he said. What are you doing?

Maybe I'm coming down with something, I said.

What does it feel like?

My back was heavy. It feels I wanted to say like thirty-five years came into my body and forgot to leave. There's too much time in here. I'm done for.

Aching muscles, I said. He snorted and went out. A bit later I heard him shout, It's not in the laundry bin or the airing cupboard!

I needed to go to the shops and buy food. Buy food, I thought. That was one thing. And get up and move a bit. Move. That was another.

Should I call someone, I asked myself. Arrange to meet for a coffee? Too late notice. Weekend. Are you depressed? I feel uneasy with things. You're not getting younger. You look relatively all right now. You're relatively young. Shouldn't things be happening? Isn't this when things should happen? Is there something you forgot to do to make them start?

But the quiet part of me said there was no point forcing anything. It wouldn't work. Then what should I do? Shouldn't I do something? Is this all you want from me? I nagged. But it didn't want me to do anything. Why is everything so fucking simple? I asked, then wanted to laugh.

Jason came back in. Kick-off's in an hour! he said.

Did you look in your bag? I said.

He went away. Got it! I heard.

By the way there's no food, he said when he came back in, wearing his tracksuit, bag slung over his shoulder. I had cereal. I'm just telling you. I can go to the shop on my way back but it'll be later. Text me if you want me to. Bye Mum.

Bye, I said, and I went back to trying to understand something about the day, and what it wanted.

7

Waiting

The hardest times passed like fire. I don't remember much till Jason was two. Till he was at school. I used to think of this documentary they showed when we were in school. It was a woman talking about World War Two. Her hair was set in white curls like Nan's, her face a map of wrinkles. You saw a photograph of her before, a young woman, round-cheeked, wearing lipstick, and wondered how she'd let herself get old.

The door again, he was back. I heard coughing panting kicking off his trainers and chucking his keys on the counter.

The old lady said something, her eyes sparkling. About the war. Ooh it was a difficult time but a wonderful time. There were love affairs. You never knew what was going to happen so you didn't think about tomorrow. You just lived. Her face shone.

That was how it was when Jason was a baby or I first started work or looked after him when he was ill. There wasn't that terrible sadness I used to feel when I was a girl standing on the common knee-deep in grass on a cloudy summer day looking at a line of trees waiting just waiting for something to happen.

In the other room he was breathing lighting up putting on the kettle. His phone beeped. Sometimes I think if I had long enough to sit and think I'd understand what to do, how to get out of the grass and move ahead.

We still hadn't talked about it properly, college, and next year – what he was going to do.

All right, he said, when I went into the kitchen. He didn't look up from putting peanut butter on his toast. The knife went down on the counter. I imagined picking it up later, wiping the counter, washing the knife. Getting the kitchen clean, which it wouldn't stay.

Jason, have you had a chance to think about college? I said. I picked up the knife and laid it across the open jar.

He breathed out harder and put down the plate. I'm just having some food, he said.

I know you are, I said. He leaned back against the counter and stared at the wall.

I don't want you to miss out, I said.

No chance of that, he said.

I'm not having a go, I said. Sound of him chomping, crumbs everywhere. He finished the toast and put in another slice.

I might not want to go to college, he said. I might get a job.

Oh Jason, I said. If you don't go to college you're just stupid.

He yanked up the toaster lever and the bread popped. He walked out. That didn't come out right. I stood there buzzing with things I wanted to explain, waiting for him to return. Music came out of the closed door of his room, something thumping. After a bit I washed the knife, wiped up the crumbs and the peanut butter, disliked myself for doing it.

8

People want everything to look perfect

The curtains at work are striped, ticking I think Nan would have called it: light blue with a few other colours, yellow, white, navy, pink. Pretty. The windows on our side face west. The morning light comes in the other side. I was spraying the heels on a stand of wedding shoes, covering my face because the spray catches in your throat, and when I looked up sunlight was coming through a window on to the trolley, and the spray was caught in a cloud, slowly dancing.

It's always warm on the floor, and in summer it's sweaty. The compressor stopped working because of a fault. While we waited for them to fix it we became slower, like bumble bees on a hot afternoon. We did what we could by hand. Tom worked on his lasts. He smiled. You know, lass, this is how we used to do it, he said, in the old days. And we'd be fast.

I know, I said. It was piecework.

It was piecework, he said.

That's what Nan used to talk about, I said. No time to hang about.

I never took any days' leave, do you know that? he said. Maybe three or four in thirty years of piecework. There was a week when I started. I think it was the chemicals. I got really sick but I didn't take a day off. I was going in with a fever.

His hands were working while he talked, pulling tight the leather around the last, hammering it in place. What is it, I thought, about this work; the same thing, over and over, it takes your life but in the process it gives you this quietness, it takes away the struggle. Or maybe that's just Tom. Or what I see of Tom from the outside.

You're quiet today, Claire, John said. He smiled at me. I smiled back. He's a bit older than me, John, but probably not much. He's nice, too – smiles, and follows me with his eyes. We don't talk a lot, except if we're outside smoking. He always looks the same: jeans and t-shirts, his hair cut like it probably was twenty years ago, close and smooth.

Just checking what I can do till the compressor starts, I said. I like talking to Tom, and I don't like it when people come along. It's not even that I'm telling Tom private things. It's just a way of being.

John smiled and went back to his work. He was using his hands too, but more slowly than Tom. It would mostly have been machines when he started.

I went to see Derek at the heel attacher. He was hammering in nails by hand to fix the heels on Eveliina, a red high heel, strappy. One I'd almost wear, if I had somewhere to wear it. Maybe I'll try it in the factory shop. But what for?

Jane had sent down six boxes of handbags to have them checked and freshened up. We don't make them, but we sell them as part of the line. The girls and I opened the plastic, took out the bags, checked them for marks, and stuffed them with tissue so they didn't look crushed. In the shop, people want everything to look perfect.

Does that even look better? I asked Ellie. I held out the bag, plumped out. That looks the same, doesn't it?

But she said that looked better.

Just before lunch the compressor started again and we all stopped doing the things we'd been doing to keep busy and we worked and worked. It was the busyness again the radio the noise of the machines the smell of leather dust and all of us working without mind, like bees in a hive. I didn't think till just after four when I thought, I've had enough, that's enough of today. The last twenty minutes crept by but when we were walking out it was still bright and hazy and everyone was chattering about what they were going to do tonight. Helen's husband came to meet her like he always does – he's retired. But not in the car, because the weather was so fine. He took her hand and she went off pink-cheeked and smiling like a little girl and the pair of them over sixty. How's that done, I thought, but I liked it.

9

When I'm tired

On the way home I stopped and sat on the wall near the shop, just to be in the sun. There were three kids messing around next to the bottle bank. The littlest reminded me of Katie. He had expressions on his face that must have come from other people: his stepdad, his older brother: a toughness, a blankness, that didn't belong to him. Then he scowled, and looked for a minute like an older woman, maybe his mum. It's like you come into the world a person, with something it means to be you. In no time – a few years – you're carrying all these things you borrowed, like I started chewing my lip because Jim did. Those habits become what people meet in you.

When I'm tired things are clear. It takes the edge off. I feel like a saint in a stained-glass window, everything coming to me in a halo, revelations.

I shut my eyes and turned my face up. Orange. Red thread

veins. Little things like bacteria moving. My body sleepy with a private hum like one of the machines.

Hi. Excuse me, someone said.

I opened my eyes. Everything yellow and blue, like a seventies film. A shirt, white, slim fit, tucked in. Brown trousers. Brogues, nice ones. Up again, slowly. He was standing close.

Sorry to disturb you. (A golden voice. It had a softness it knew would please.) Do you have a light?

His wrist, golden hairs, brown canvas watchstrap. The man from the pub.

Yeah, I said.

While I was looking for it he waited. He put out his hand. Thanks, he said. I watched him look down and light his cigarette. He inhaled, didn't give me the lighter. Didn't I see you in the Three Bells the other day? he said easily. In the garden?

Oh! Oh, yeah, probably, I said. What day was that?

He smiled. I'm not sure, he said. Few days ago. Wasn't as nice as today.

It's lovely, isn't it?

It is. He smoked. I got out my tin and started rolling.

He sat next to me on the wall to light it. Held on to the lighter, looked at it. I'd smelled his hand, nicotine and skin. It's nice to smoke when it's hot. Some days I want to smoke because something at work's already irritated my throat. It's like having a tooth that's loose, or a cut that's closing.

What about a half in the Bells? he said. If you have time.

I tried not to smile because the first thing I thought was but this never happens to me.

Now? I said.

Why not? he said.

Could do.

At the Bells we, Damian and me, smoked a lot. He bought the first drink. That's when I found out his name. He handed me my beer and said, I'm Damian by the way. Claire, I said, but he didn't hear because we were walking out to the garden. It was nearly full.

Sorry, he said.

Claire, I said again.

Beer garden, it's one of those phrases, like holiday home, it tells you you're meant to be having a good time. I did a quick scan but didn't see anyone I knew. Damian seemed comfortable. He rolled up his sleeves and put his arms on the table.

So, Claire, do you live round here?

I live with my son. Up the road. He's sixteen, I said quickly. I always say it fast, because I don't want to have to think about it later.

He nodded. What's his name?

Jason.

Jason and the Argonauts, he said.

You didn't say Jason Donovan, I said.

Is he named after Jason Donovan?

No.

That's good, he said. He laughed. I used to have the piss ripped out of me at school for looking like him.

You don't really, though, I said. He is blond, but his face isn't the same. Blue eyes but a bit more round. He looks like a kid, especially when he laughs.

I used to hate my name, he said. Everyone made fun of it. People thought I was posh.

Are you?

He looked down, shook his head.

You don't have an accent, I said.

Moved around a bit, he said. His eyes asked for understanding. Tell me about you, Claire, he said.

I turned my glass around. Not much to say, I said. Born and brought up here. I looked around the beer garden. Sometimes I feel like I'm not from here, I said. That I've moved around too. But I've never lived anywhere else.

He nodded. Got lots of family here?

I don't see them much, I said. I noticed I was holding my glass tightly. I took a big sip, had to wipe my chin.

Damian nodded. He was just listening, accepting what I said.

What about your family? I asked.

He smiled, waved his right hand. All over the place, you know, he said. Here and there.

Right.

And what do you do, Claire?

I work at a shoe factory, I said. Up near Ketts Hill.

Oh, really? That's interesting.

There were twenty or more factories at one time, I said. Loads of people worked in the shoe trade. I felt like a tourist guide.

I think I'd heard that, he said. He took his sunglasses out of his pocket and put them on. I felt relieved. People usually think it's weird, or they say, I didn't realise there were any shoe factories left.

What do you do? I asked.

He smiled. For a moment I saw my head in the glasses, distorted, waving.

I sell children's books, Claire. I'm a rep. I travel round and talk to bookshops about our titles. And schools. Books for little kids, he said. Not Jason's age.

I didn't mind hearing him say Jason's name. Normally I don't like it when someone I don't know uses it.

He'd finished his drink. My arms were cold. I rubbed them. On the road, I heard traffic. It was beginning to turn into evening. A few more people filtered into the garden. Shall I get another? I asked.

Can't, he said. Got to go, meeting some people. He got up sudden and I did too. Can I give you a lift? he said. The car's just round the corner.

Oh no, I said. It's only a minute.

Well, see you again, Claire, he said, as though we met up every week. And he left. He still had my lighter, I realised when I got in.

10

There was weather

A funny day when inside and outside weren't as separate as normal. What'll happen next, I thought. What's going to happen? Partly about Damian. Nothing, said my mind. That was it. He had an hour to kill in between things probably. I thought of my face without any make-up, and my t-shirt and jeans, and felt no confidence.

Chris who works the drying machine wasn't in and I've done that job before, so I worked it all day. One of the styles we've been making for the past few days, the red heel, it was coming through from the rougher. The flat shoe in the rubber cradles looks like a woman's body. The part after the instep has a shape, like hips. But it just lies there, upside down, a sad fish. It's only when the heel gets put on that it looks like anything.

I worked on the dryer, then glued on the soles with the

attached heels, put them on a trolley to pass to John so he could fix the heels. I like John, how he's calm, often looks amused. When we smoke he's friendly, chats, remembers things I've said. A pouch of tobacco and a packet of papers sit next to the box of nails on the side of the heel attacher. I sometimes pinch a fag from him at break.

It rained all day. Not heavy but it was colder. I'd forgotten the forecast and come to work in sandals. With the sound of the rain and the chill near the windows, and smelling the glue as the shoes came out of the dryer, and looking at the pictures of mountains that Chris has stuck on the side – he likes climbing, he and his wife go on walking holidays – I forgot to wonder what was going to happen.

At four thirty there was still weather. I had to walk home in it, and listen to my feet squelch, feel them slide. I smoked a sad cigarette in the rain, dirty fumes and chilled fingers. It makes my kidneys cold, this weather, Nan used to say. I got in. The kitchen needed cleaning. The house was cold. I put on the lights it was that dark. The bin needed taking out. Everything smelled damp. Nothing would happen, it was obvious. Everything was just the way it was, the only way it ever would be.

11

The smell of the ink

I knocked on his door. Hip hop coming out but quietly. Knocked again.

I SAID YEAH!

I pushed open the door, went in, smiled. He was lying on the floor drawing, a cigarette next to him in an Indian metal ashtray someone from school gave him. I clocked some King Size Rizlas on the shelf above the bed, the end of the packet torn.

Your clothes, I said.

Thanks, he said. He didn't look up. I heard the scratch of a Rotring. For a minute I stood looking at the back of his head, his biceps in his blue t-shirt, the looseness of his jeans under the waist, the instep of one foot in a stripy sock.

He cocked his head, wondered silently why I was still there. All right? he offered.

I bent down and kissed the warm whorl at the crown of his head. An absent-minded big hand came out, patted my calf, carried on drawing a line of buildings – some tall, some with spires, pointed roofs.

Do you want me to close the door, I asked like an idiot.

He nodded, didn't look up. Thanks, Mum.

When I gave birth and saw Jason was a boy, I cried. I knew if I had a girl she'd hate me.

I remember when he was about three there was something I wouldn't let him do. I forget what. He stood in the middle of the room and screamed,

I hate you! I hate you! I hate you!

You'd think I'd have been upset, but I wasn't. I felt like swinging him into the air and spanking him and shouting, I hate you more! A thrill went through me. I saw myself doing it.

I should have hugged him, but I left the room and had a fag and thought about what a horrible little world it is. When I came back he'd fallen over, or hit his head. He was crying, and I cuddled him. I felt sorry for him, for both of us.

He stopped crying. He was holding on to my top with one fist and he leaned away and stared at me, all weary, like an old person. As though he was saying, Oh, I get it, this is what it's like? This is it? We looked at each other.

One of the worst things I did was when he was old enough to have a key and come home from school on his own. I was back to doing full days. He must have been ten or eleven.

We'd had an argument all weekend, about these football boots he wanted, which Ronaldo wore. They were gold and cost a fortune. I told him he already had perfectly functional boots and he became furious and said he needed them.

I got back and he was sitting in the middle of the lounge tearing something. It looked like there was grey water all over the floor. The ripped-up sports sections. He must have been at it for an hour.

He looked up at me, distracted, like he'd gone into another place, though he must have been angry when he started.

I said, Jason, what have you done?

I imagined screaming, What have you done? What the fuck have you done? You stupid boy! I'm going to kill you!

I stood on the edge of the sea of newsprint. Then I said very quietly, One of these days I'm going to leave. I'll just go. You'll get back and I won't be here. And I won't ever come back.

He looked at me with his mouth open. As though he'd suspected I was mad but couldn't believe it.

I sat down, closed my eyes and said I was sorry, and I'd never do that. He said, It's all right, Mum, but I think he meant, Don't cry, you're only crying for yourself. I remember that with my mother, her hitting me and then crying.

I sat down in the paper.

What are you doing? he said.

I'm tired, I said. And I was, I realised. I lay down.

Mum!

Close the door, I said.

I lay there while it got dark, maybe for an hour. I thought about my grandpa and how he'd say I was having a reaction. I remembered sleeping between them, him and Nan, in their bed. In the night if I tried to get close to Grandpa he'd turn away. But I'd cuddle up to Nan's back and a big arm would come over me and pat my bum. I'd be warm. I'd hear next door's dog or a dog in the street howl and I'd think that's the sound of loneliness. I'll always remember that sound I'd think. After a while of lying there and crying I thought about how old I was now – thirty years old. I'm thirty years old, I thought, with my cheek in newsprint. It smelled cheap, the ink. I wondered if I'd have black smears on my face, or half a word. From an ad. SALE, but backwards. I was cold, and hungry, and it was dark. I needed a wee. I got up, turned on the light, picked up the paper, made us fish fingers and chips, and went to the corner shop for ice cream. I gave Jason a hug before and told him I did love him. He let me hug him and said he knew.

While I was on my way to the shop I had a smoke. I felt done in, like I'd been crying for days. I thought to myself something I often thought at that time when anything went wrong, whatever it was, and then when it stopped, at least for a bit: Well, that passed the time. And then I'd laugh, really laugh, because no one else would have understood.

12

Sunny delight

An arm out of the window, sleeve rolled up, sun shining on the golden hair. Dark glasses, a face: Claire, he said. Give you a lift?

Oh, hiya, I said.

Hop in.

I hopped in. We were off.

He gave me a big smile. Hello, sunny delight, he said.

I laughed. What did you just call me?

He smiled and pushed his sunglasses up his nose. In a hurry? he asked.

No, I said. I felt wonderful, like everything had opened up.

Let's go for a little drive, he said.

I saw familiar things: the shop, the pub, the hill, and houses I see every day – one at the corner with an apple tree and a hedge, and a white one with a conservatory and a sharp-leaved plant near the door. But they passed by fast, and then they were gone.

In the end he parked not too far from the house, and we went for a walk in Lion Wood. Lots of couples here and there on seats. We walked through the clearing, where the sun hung in slow soft bars, and up into one of the bits with more trees, then we were alone.

Well, Claire, he said. He looked at me and smiled, waiting.

I had questions I wanted to ask, things I wanted to say, like, I didn't think I'd see you again, how did you know when I'd be walking past, where have you been for the last month – but instead he kissed me. It was too fast. I was still thinking. His tongue was in my mouth, his hands were on my arse, then touching my breasts, in my hair, pulling it. I opened my eyes. His face looked different, blind. He put my hand on his trousers and I felt his hard-on. He sighed. Voices, and three kids came up the path. They giggled as they passed.

Casey! one said, and shoved a skinny boy.

Oh, I love you, I love you, he whined and pushed her back.

Damian moved away from me. He took out his tobacco, papers, filters, sat down and began to roll.

I sat near him and did the same. He didn't speak, he seemed further away than he was. The sunlight fell through the trees, and got lost before it could reach the ground.

Well, he said, best be getting back, I suppose. You probably need to get back, don't you. He seemed to have lost energy.

Not really, I said. But I did. I hadn't said anything to Jason.

Let's get you home, he said. We didn't talk on the way.

When he dropped me at the corner he said, So when am I going to see you again? He said he often went to the Star, nearer town, on a Friday night. Will I see you there? he asked.

What time?

Oh, later, he said. About eight. Eight or so. So long then.

He drove off and I went towards the house, doing things to my hair.

Jason was home, with Steve. They were making tea – potato waffles, baked beans, fish fingers. He put more on. I sat at the table with a cup of tea. The kitchen was light, a good smell in the air, the back door open, summer coming in. Something white and grey flitted across the edge of my eye. I turned. The cat from up the road – it likes our garden.

Steve smiled at me. How are you, Claire? he asked. He's a nice lad. There's something damp about his eyes, but he has a sweet smile.

I'm all right, I said. How's it going? How's your mum?

I was going to ask about his plans for next year, college or what, but then I thought better. A good day, why not just let it be a good day.

13

He doesn't look like his dad

Jason and I needed to talk about next year. I didn't remember when we'd had a conversation that lasted longer than a few minutes and didn't end with him walking off. I watched him eating his tea tonight, but he didn't look at me. He knew I wanted to talk; I knew he didn't.

He doesn't look that much like his dad, thank God. Except his colouring. There was an age – when he was eleven, twelve – when he looked just like Pete. It was strange – the first man I'd been with appearing from time to time in my son. Pete wasn't even a man when we started up. We were kids, but we thought we were grown up. He looked older, more like a man, around the time he left. It hurt for so long. Now I can't believe how young we were – almost Jason's age.

Jason's the same build as Pete now – tall, broad in the shoulder, not like me. The same dark hair and blue eyes. But he reminds me more of Jim, Jim who isn't there any more. I used to tell him when he looked like someone. Now I don't bother. He doesn't like it. He's good at shaking things off, Jason. He doesn't have to say anything. He just looks across, like a little bull, eyes big and direct, and gets ready to refuse.

But he did say something, just before he took his plate to the sink. Mum, some of the lads are going to Newquay in August.

Oh right? I said.

For a week or ten days. Staying in a hostel. I want to go.

Do you, I said. I find myself saying stupid things, like my mum, when I don't want to say yes but I don't know how not to.

Can I? For my birthday? He stopped and looked at me straight. He was properly asking.

When are they leaving?

The fifth or so.

Can't you come back for your birthday? I was thinking of having a party. You could have your friends round.

He didn't quite roll his eyes.

Why am I always trying to stop him, I thought.

We could have it when I get back, he said. Couple of days later.

Like the nineteenth or twentieth? All right, I said. Have you got enough money?

Yeah yeah, he said. He had his back to me. He was even washing the plate. Nearly, he said.

How much do you need?

Maybe a hundred and fifty quid.

Early birthday present, eh? I said.

He turned round and grinned at me. His grin can floor you, that boy. Thanks, Mum, he said.

I went to the bedroom and tried not to think about Jason battered out of his mind in Newquay and the stories you read in the paper. I'd make him text me every day. Because that'd help. It always went like this. I said no no no no oh okay then. I didn't want to be that parent, the one who says no and doesn't know what happens. Not that anyone knows.

And this wasn't why I'd said yes, I swear, but I also thought: the house empty for ten days.

14

A spotlight

He turned me over. Here, he said. He put a pillow next to me.

What? I said. I looked at him over my shoulder. The curtains were drawn. I couldn't see his face. He was kneeling over me.

Put it under you. Here. He helped me shift it, then got into me. There you go, he murmured as he started moving. He said things to himself. Yeah … Mmm … and got turned on quickly. Do you want me to come? he asked.

I thought it was a general question. Course, I said. He moved faster and did, with a shout. When he'd finished, he breathed in and moved in me a few times, just I guess because it felt good.

I waited for him to say something about the fact that I hadn't come, offer to do something. He leaned back, took the pillow from me, put his head on it, got me in the crook of his arm. I liked that, the warmth. He'd be here for a while; he was in no hurry. And it was still early. I looked up at him, but he was different. Before, he was concentrated on me, like a spotlight. Now, he was here, my head was on his chest, but I'd disappeared.

He looked up at the ceiling. So, Claire, he said, how do you like doing it?

How do you mean? I said. I like it, I added.

He chuckled. His chest moved under my face.

What?

You're funny, he said. He squeezed me with his arm. No, I meant, which way? Which other way do you like?

Like, position?

Mm.

I don't know, I said. Er, from behind, sideways. I felt depressed, like in school when people would ask, What's your favourite band, and you knew there was a right or wrong answer.

He looked down at me, interested. Embarrassed? he said.

Not embarrassed, I said. It's just weird, talking about it.

Not embarrassed, but it's weird talking about it, he repeated. He stretched his free arm towards the bedside table, looked at his watch, put it on his wrist.

What time is it? I said.

I've got a bit of time, he said.

I put my arm over his stomach. Under the curtain I could see the colour of the light, going from orangey to golden.

Maybe it was around five thirty, six. When I'd got his text that afternoon I'd rushed home, taken a shower, waited for him. He usually left around six. Somehow he never ran into Jason. I didn't plan it, or have to try.

Did I ever tell you about Lisa? he said. He put his free arm behind his head, looked up at the ceiling.

Lisa?

She was my first proper girlfriend, in school.

Oh, I said. No, you didn't.

We were fifteen. We used to hang out at her house after school. Both her parents worked so we – she had a key.

Right.

He stroked my arm. She was so beautiful, he said. A really sexy girl. I didn't know anything then – neither of us did. His voice was dreamy. He looked down at me suddenly. We did everything, he said. He laughed. We even got a book out of the library, can you imagine?

I smiled. He was looking at me but I wasn't me. He was still talking and I began thinking, remembering how I'd felt in the afternoon, knowing I was going to have sex in a few hours. The smell of the machines and the oil giving me a headache, and being turned on, it reminded me of school, when I'd just started secondary. Sex had arrived then, for all of us – not that I was having sex yet, but all of a sudden it was there. There was a while, a few months, when it was all I could think of. I'd do it to myself whenever I could. A few times in a cubicle in the loo. It took no trying. Things were happening to all of us – breasts, hair on our legs, the boys starting to get spots and shave. For some reason, though, I thought I was the only one having this experience, this dirty but amazing secret.

15

This is better

It had been so long that I'd forgotten what it was like, but in the last few weeks I felt again that there was someone in the world who heard me. As though I could make a call, like a bird, and after a while someone would return it. Sometimes I'd be thinking of Damian and then I'd hear from him: magic.

The first day after I'd seen him I woke up feeling downy, cushioned, like a chick in a nest. There was nothing I needed. I felt more patient. Work was easier. Jason had gone out leaving some things – papers, a plate, a pan – on the table, more stuff in the lounge. I tidied up without thinking. While I was doing it, picking up socks from the blue velvet couch, a bit like the one we'd had at home when I was a kid, I thought maybe I should go and see Dad. Jason went to see them a month ago. He looks tired, Jason told me. He stopped,

I remember, and took a drag on his fag. I hate him smoking, but I can't say anything. He said, He looks like he's drying up, Mum. He looks smaller.

I should go and see them, I thought. I patted the sofa cushions. I thought of Mum at the bakery, and fixing it up with her, a time to drop round, and her face, fat with anger, and I thought I would.

The second day, I started to think about Damian. When would I see him next? I made a bet with myself. If I saw two people wearing a red top between the factory door and the top of Plumstead Road, I'd see him tomorrow. If I – Sometimes I'd be right. This time the days passed. Three, four, five. I waited. He called, said impatiently, Sorry I haven't been around for a bit. I said it's fine. I know you're busy. He seemed to relax.

It was in the back of my mind, anyway, Jason being away in a few weeks, and the lovely time Damian and I would have. It'd be easy. So I waited. Things would get better. That Friday I was walking home, a beautiful sunny afternoon. Ahead of me down the hill the cathedral spire was pale gold in a blue sky. The world had never had any problems. I thought, everyone has something, something they need from other people. Some people want to be loved. Some want to be admired. Some people just need to know you don't need them to be any way other than they are. I was calm, except when I wasn't. I felt good. I'm learning, I thought, as I walked in the sunshine. It was different from other things, like with Pete, Jason's dad.

It's simpler to think of him that way, Jason's dad, an abstract person that I don't see. It was all fire, and we were so young. When I found out I was pregnant he decided he'd go away to work. He said he might join the army. Later I heard he'd gone to America. His family wasn't from round here, and they moved soon after. For a while he sent things for Jason, but not for long, a couple of years. A card on his birthday, and a present, for a while after that. Even that stopped ages ago. It was stupid, a mistake. But I got Jason out of it.

I got to our gate, opened it, and the fat cat from down the road miaowed and scurried out. Oh hello, I said. It hurried up the street, dodging under cars.

Things were different with Damian. It was quieter, slower. We hadn't said anything about the future. But when we were together it felt simple, easy. This is better, I thought.

16

Autumn couldn't ever come

I sat just outside the storm and waited. It's the only way. I pretended to read yesterday's *Evening News* and drink a cup of tea but the tea got cold and I read and reread one caption: Eleven-year-old Hayley Adams is delighted to have been named the winner of … Photo of her, long hair, ambitious eyes, asking life, What have you got to offer me? Some kids give me the willies.

I wiped the table and cleaned the kitchen floor. I rolled a cigarette but didn't light it. Jason kept coming in, asking about: his blue jumper, his football socks, his phone charger, no, wait, he had it, no, did I have it? Had I been using his fucking phone charger again? All that. Steve arrived, smiled at me. How are you, Claire? Nice to see you.

I found it funny, nice though, Sandra's done a good job hasn't she, or is Jason this smooth with other people's mothers, probably. Jason came in the kitchen with his football holdall over his shoulder, shades on. Bye, Mum, he said, and gave me a hug.

I stood there staring at him. Had his voice gone deeper? Was he taller? Text me, I said.

Yeah yeah, he said. Definitely. He winked as he closed the door. If I don't it only means I've run out of credit. He and Steve passed the glass, a blur of blue and laughter.

Well don't run out of credit then, I said to the door. It blew open. The air outside was warm. I stood in the back yard and had my rollie and watched the leaves wave on the tree next door – an apple tree. Little green fruit turning colour. But the sky was blue and high. Autumn couldn't ever come, not for a long time. When I'd finished smoking and had that ashy, restful feeling I turned back. I'd get the house ready and then get in touch with Damian.

17

The cars carried on passing

It felt good to clean. I bought flowers, tidied up the back garden – picked up the crisp packets that blow in, cut the edges of the grass. Swept the patio. We might sit out in the morning for breakfast. I tidied the lounge, the bedroom, changed the sheets and put on the soft cotton ones I'd bought a month ago, vacuumed. The windows were open. I smelled flowers, the exhaust of a car going past, heard voices floating on the warm air.

When I was tired and empty, beginning to be hungry, I texted Damian to ask if he wanted to come over. I said I had the house to myself. I put a kiss on the end. I carried on, waiting, doing things. I hung out the sheets. The back door was open. The sheets were bigger than me. I liked stretching to straighten them on the line. I'd hear my phone when the reply came. The same noises from outside and, when I went in, the hum of the fridge. In the apple tree a blackbird, making its call that sounded like water, a song sung through liquid.

I took a shower, put on my new dress and perfume, went out to get bread, eggs, bacon, and orange juice. Walked slowly back from the shop, not looking at my phone. Unpacked things, put away the bag, threw the receipt into the empty lined bin. The kitchen smelled of kitchen cleaner. The floors smelled of floor cleaner. The cars carried on passing. In the afternoon it got greyer, a bit colder. I left the windows open. There was no reply, no reply at all.

18

That feeling

Was it real, this feeling, or just a fear, the old one, that everything was ruined?

This can't be happening, I kept thinking. But the heaviness in my stomach said it was.

On Sunday I was awake till early morning. Rain, wind. The house was still, just the hum of the fridge. I wanted to put on the heating. I got dressed, had tea, smoked out the back door. I looked in the fridge at the bacon and eggs. Yellow and red stripes on the bacon packet, dates: Sell by, Use by … There's time, I thought. I texted Jason, Rainy here, hope the weather's still good in Newquay. No reply. Maybe he was out, maybe it was still sunny there. My son on a beach with his friends, girls, cans of beer, the sun, their shoulders burning. I fried an egg and looked at it, white, shiny, a brown curl at the edge. When it was cold, I broke the yolk with the end of a knife. Tilted the plate, watched it drool, yellow goo. Drank a glass of orange juice. This couldn't be happening. I lay on the sofa with the light on.

Monday came, and it was the same as always. I hadn't slept much, slept in bits, waking to argue in my head with Damian, who didn't say anything back, just smiled and smoked, or got in his car and drove away, slowly.

19

Alphabetti spaghetti

Claire?

Funny how someone can sound annoyed before a conversation even starts.

Yeah, I said. I looked at the cordless then put it back to my ear. Who's this?

Sharp sucking in. It's Alison. Paul's wife.

I still think of Paul as my other brother, even though he's the only one left.

Yeah? I said. How's things? A stupid question but I didn't know what to say. I don't like her ringing. For that matter, I don't like her. She's got a sharp face and a smile that looks like it's hurting her.

Another inbreath. Claire, she started, I'm sorry but I've got bad news. It's about your dad.

She went on, in a rush but careful, like a kid in a school

play who got a bigger part than she was expecting. A whole speech. I let her get through it and while she was talking I sat on the third step from the bottom looking at the coloured glass in the front door. The pale blue pane, my favourite. I used to sit here when I was a kid and it was Grandpa and Nan's house, staring at the blue, which looked like water you could dive into.

Alison answered the questions I would have asked, like when, what happened, how long had he been feeling ill, how long did it take.

Your mum said she told Jason he wasn't well, she threw in.

I picked at the cuticle of my right middle finger and didn't say anything.

We'll be in touch, she said. About the arrangements. It likely won't be for a week at least. I expect you'll want to come and see your mum.

After a while I said, Let me know when it is. Jason's away so I need to tell him in time.

She said something, I don't know what, and I put down the phone. The hallway was dark, at the end of it a rectangle of light and some birds singing. I went towards the back garden and rolled up. The first person I thought about was Damian. Maybe this'd make him come back? Then Jason. I phoned but his phone was off. I sent a message: Please call as soon as you can, love Mum. He'd be back in two days. We'd talked the day before yesterday, on his birthday.

The sky was still high and blue. The sun was warm.

I wondered if I should get drunk. It was nearly six, and I could smell someone's barbecue. I was hungry. There was Dad, dead in an undertaker's somewhere. I wished I'd asked which one. Alison would have given me the details. She must have loved all this, silly bitch. Or maybe she didn't. Why don't you stop being so angry with everyone, I told myself, and carried on smoking. I imagined things I could eat. Sausages. Baked beans on toast. Alphabetti spaghetti. Hadn't had that in the house in years. Salad with salad cream. Food that came in packets, in portions, so you couldn't get it wrong. I lay on the grass. It was damp and cool. The lawn was shagged, I hadn't looked after it. It was tufty in some places, bald in others. The sun had moved, and the grass was mostly in the shade, but there was sun in my eyes. I shut them. Managed a tear. Smells of earth, grass, meat on a barbecue, someone's perfume or deodorant, petrol. Summer smells. A radio. Soon I'd roll another cigarette.

20

Ash

I didn't tell anyone at work. And I felt fine. Sometimes I'd think about him, at the undertaker's in a coffin, his face strange. They do things to you, don't they? Make you look nice. Waxy like Red Delicious apples used to be. He still existed in the world but he couldn't move. He was like a stopped watch, one of the ones with wavy edges around the face and a leather strap, pretending to be more expensive than it is. When Mum said or did something to me, he'd pat me on the head after. He knew how I felt. He just didn't do anything.

It was warm. I worked as fast as ever – faster than some days. The sun came through the high windows and in the afternoon the light bathed my station. We were working on Grace, a wedding shoe, white satin with a diamanté buckle. Spoils easily. I had to take one or two back to the sewing machines to show Helen and Karen. Most of them were fine.

I matched them up, this with that, that with this, rearranging them so they made perfect pairs. Put them on the trolley for Tracy to wrap and box.

On the way home my cigarette tasted of ash and I thought that's what a dead body tastes like. Right there, next to the kerb, I was being sick. It was hours after I'd eaten, so only a bit of water came out, frothy and sour. I got myself straightened up and looked round, but no one had seen or cared. I wiped my mouth, swallowed and carried on down the road.

II

Chappals

1

A small temple

During the time when I was drinking I had dreams of great colour and violence. I didn't always remember them, but I'd wake knowing that something had been happening, like sleeping in a room where the television has been on. There was one I had regularly. Sometimes it was in the hall of a railway station, a big one, like CST in Mumbai. Under the arches and pillars it felt like a maidan. I was on the ground, watching people pass. I saw their calves – the men's thin and dark, with sandals at the end, or heavy rubber chappals, and the women's, legs emerging from a nine-yard sari, sometimes a regular sari, a girl's legs in jeans, toe rings on her feet. The steps crossed and recrossed without anyone colliding even when it seemed they must and I watched now one pair of feet then another waiting for them to stop or clash but they only went on. The sound of the steps was regular and organic, like rain.

This morning again I had the dream. This time it was in the courtyard of the old Rajwada. People came and went, passing and crossing one another, and I was at the side, where the bartan sellers sit with their new, well-made pans, or the old woman inside the gate, with her basket of flowers. I woke not remembering who I was, or where, still looking for all those feet.

The metal at the top of the bed was cold. The room was damp and dark. I thought of a shower over a green vegetable field, with a small temple at the end. I saw myself bending to pray at the lintel, hardly seeing the surrounding fields as rain smudged them out. But I wasn't in a field of cucumber vines; I was here in the city. At the other end of the room the cat was watching me. I cursed silently, and got up.

This afternoon I was hammering the soles I'd cut in the morning. She sat next to me, using scraps of hide to cut out decorations: sharp-petalled flowers that she stamped with a die. I listened to the silence, the road outside, and from the back the birds. The rain smelled fresh, but inside the damp mixed with the smell of the hides. When it was time for tea, before she went to the kitchen she put on the radio.

This is the Voice of Heaven. And now on the Voice of Heaven you'll hear the news in Marathi. The Prime Minister has said …

The cat rose from the corner. He yawned, stretched out his forearms, then his legs, one foot at a time in the air. He sat on his haunches, glaring at me, sleepy and bad-tempered as though he'd only just remembered his condition in life. Then he wandered out. Rascal, badmash, shaitan, I said, and as he passed he leaned on me, heavy and friendly like a drunk.

Eh, Tukoba! my wife called from the kitchen. Then, because he didn't stop, Tukaram Maharaj!

Someone could take offence, I suppose, but no one has. Perhaps it's age. The old, like the drunk, are judged differently. I don't really believe cats have names, but she, this one, insisted we name him, and so on a whim I said Tuka. I don't know much about poets, or saints, or cats for that matter. During my drinking years, when he was young, this cat was good at getting out of the way, so we never lost respect for each other.

She handed me my tea. You and that cat, she said.

I stood at the door, looking at him looking out. He sat blinking and washing his face until something moved – a bird, a flash of colour. Then he went with purpose into the yard.

I left for my walk. It's not that I've given up drinking, I say to myself in the evenings. I'm just not drinking right now. How long has it been? Nine years? Ten? The sun was gone, the light was becoming blue. It's one of my two favourite times of day, a sadness as the electric lights come on and the air holds the smell of dhoop and woodsmoke. The leaves of the trees blacken, and birds fly up, calling to each other.

Pawar! Arun! I thought I heard as I passed the bottle shop.

I kept walking, but I put out a hand to wave. Borkar.

When I returned home, I heard the radio, Bhimsen Joshi's familiar voice blaring out, a voice I've never specially cared for. I could see the light through the door, which was a little ajar.

2

Is it time?

Is it time to go? These days I'm sure I need to, and I get up in the night, and go out to the latrine. But I have difficulty beginning.

There's a sense of urgency, but it'll start, then stop. During these excursions, still dreaming I suppose, I believe I am at home, I mean the house where I grew up. A boy, stumbling into moonlight. In the room where I slept as a child, the walls smelled of ash and cow dung, smoky and rich. If you haven't been in a room plastered with gobar I can't explain. It's sweet, but catches in the back of your throat. Now, in the rains, the smell alters, a growing thing.

My brother and I slept in the corner. His knee in my leg, my foot on his calf, his snoring. The light from the window and shadows moved near us. Sometimes we had to listen to our parents' soft noises. In the morning he stirred earlier, unclouded. I had to be shaken awake, confused, often angry.

My younger daughter-in-law tells her son, Rohan, to love his brother, to look after him. We were never told such things. When we fought, if it wasn't out of sight, we were beaten for giving trouble. When we hated each other, which was often, we still slept entangled, resenting it, my knee in his back, his bony elbow in my ribs. There was no sentiment between us, but we would have died for each other.

I remember the offcuts we were given to play with. Small, oddly formed pieces. We learned to plait the leather, or stamp out a flower.

This morning I was polishing the ends of the chappals, varnishing them, checking them. Everything should be perfect. Why so much care for something a man will put between his feet and the ground? But the chappals will be his constant companions. He'll spend more time with them than with his wife. One side of the sole may wear out more, depending on how he walks, so that you could pick up his chappals and observe that he leans a little into his centre, or a little out towards the world. Some people walk quite evenly, but not many, I've noticed, not many. Most of us shuffle along in our own strange way, not giving it attention.

The thing I make is with a man when he's alone, unnoticed. He can rely on it. Our chappals aren't like the cheap manufactured ones, stuck with glue; ours will be with you for a long time.

I've never made a perfect pair. There's always something – the scorpion's tail on top of the belt curves differently on one side, or there's an asymmetry in the point of the toe.

I could say it doesn't matter, no one will notice. That the only perfect thing is a dead thing, that each pair is like a husband and wife: their imperfections complement each other.

At first it's uncomfortable to wear our chappals. They have to be lived with. When they are new, they harass the skin between your big and middle toes. You will dip them in water and let them dry in the sun. The varnish will come off the sole. You'll wear them in, slipping around. Like a tool used by the same man for years, or a child raised by a certain woman, they'll bear the imprint of your habitual bias.

My eldest son, who makes the manufactured chappals, has heard all this and isn't interested. They came this Sunday, without Anil, who had a cricket match. My daughter-in-law brought til laddoos for us to take to Pune.

Can you even remember how to make a proper chappal? I asked Prakash. I don't know why I feel the need to have these conversations with him.

He nodded, and waved one hand. His face is smooth, this son of mine, and his eyes slide around. He's darker than I, looks more like my brother.

Do you remember how? I persisted.

He smiled, but he looked irritated.

What will you teach your son? I asked.

His eyes slid up to mine, then he looked away. He exhaled. Was that last night's alcohol? His teeth are red: too much gutka.

My wife came with tea and bhajias. She put her small hand on his shoulder. He looked up and smiled, and his face changed and became absorbed, open.

If Prakash had been better in school he would have been like his younger brother, I thought, as I poured hot tea down my throat. I watched him eat, his fingers shiny with oil. He's strong, taller than I. He likes his work in the workshop with the men, and drink, and listening to songs on the radio. I don't know what else he gets up to. His wife is a practical woman, she wouldn't complain. And Anil, he's not like my other grandsons, in the city, but he's a good boy, straightforward. When his cousins come here he shows them things: the pond to swim in, or they go to the fort by bus. They look up to him, but they also turn their heads to each other and smile. His mother is always with him. They are different; they live alone, in a way. A bus takes them to school. They have a uniform, a routine.

From the cooking I smelled methi, besan, oil.

I thought about the two brothers, so different. My second son is like a version of me projected into the future. He's industrious, always wanting to get ahead, without knowing where. He has his mother's softness, her intelligence and optimism.

There's something about us that neither of them has. But not every bit of material can be used.

*

Come on, she said.

Just a minute, I said. I checked in the bag.

What now?

Did you bring the … But I couldn't come up with a word. Towels? I said.

Her eyes, lighter than mine, golden nearly, were intelligent, not quite pitying. I pulled up the zip. All right, I said. Wait – I paused. Did I need to go? No, I said. It's all right. Actually, wait. I'll be a minute.

In the bus she gazed out of the window, as though the road was telling a story. I looked across: a stall selling neera, another bus stop, people waiting in their dhotis and a man in a cap, kids in a four-wheel drive, those new hotels that have sprung up in the last ten years, all glass and signs. Everything depressed me.

What's happened to us? I felt like asking Deepak when they met us at the bus stand.

Sujata is at home, he said, finishing lunch. The boys beamed. I thought of embracing my son, and didn't. I'd shrunk. Or was he taller? He wore a short-sleeve shirt, that material with holes in it. His moustache was neatly trimmed. His mother hugged him. She never looks out of place.

You can rest while you're here, Deepak said as he opened the door of the flat. Relax, take it easy.

The house was as I remembered, white floor tiles, fans in every room. Sohan, the littler one, gave me his hand.

Do you always use the fan? I asked.

He nodded, but looked as though he wasn't sure how to answer.

What if it's cold? I said.

Then we use a sheet or a blanket, Rohan said.

There were extra mattresses, rolled up, for them to sleep on because we were there.

Baba's put the geyser on, Rohan told me, in case you want a bath.

I said nothing. Geysers make me uneasy. I shambled into the bathroom and saw myself in the mirror, an intruder with white ear hair.

In the kitchen, we sat around the table, which was covered with a shiny cloth, patterned with bright fruit: bananas, apples, tomatoes, purple plums. There were vade and tea.

You don't need to cook while you're here, Sujata told my wife. The bai comes in the morning.

My wife nodded. Then she said, Unless I make something for the boys when they come home?

Sabudana vada! said Sohan.

My daughter-in-law smiled tightly. They don't need to eat something big, she said. They normally have milk and biscuit.

Sohan squirmed on to my lap. I put an arm around him.

My son looked at me, then more closely at his mother. She was flexing her knuckles, pushing at those of the left hand. Certain joints give her pain until they warm up.

In the main room I read the newspaper. I like to see the children, and my son amid his life, which seems to fit him better than the one he had growing up. Then he was patient, watchful. Maybe that was my drinking. In the paper I read of a child being raped, in Kolhapur. I folded the paper and put it somewhere else.

It isn't that I love to be at home. But being there is no effort; I can go anywhere. Often that journey is to my childhood. The things around me are less real, but the past is immediate. When I was young I saw the future as a road. The road is still there. But this will be the last journey, one without return.

Yet the past is incomplete. My mother, for instance, isn't an image but a collection of sensations. Her hard, worn palm against my shoulder. The smell of her neck as she bent over me, smoky like a wood fire, but slightly sweet, like a water flower. When she was angry her voice rang out like a clay pot that's struck – that note of metal. Her speech sounded like an ongoing complaint, a river without variation. My father's sister was more theatrical. She laughed loudly, sat with her legs loosely crossed, and chewed supari. Even the things she did for herself, like sneezing or breathing, were amplified. In her presence I was delighted, reduced to nothing.

My father was a big man, with a big voice. He didn't speak

much, unlike my aunt, but around her he became more talkative, more smiling. I dreamed of him the other day. He was holding one chappal. He looked confused when he saw me.

Where are you off to? I said.

I'm going home, he said. But – where's your brother?

I felt the usual pang.

Is he all right? he asked. His face was full of anxiety. Better you don't tell anyone you saw me, he said, and hurried away.

3

Ghost story

When I was drinking the world became a crazy circus, entertaining and hilarious, or annoying and to be battled.

If I could just be alone. I'd think about it while I was working, hands busy, but mind elsewhere. When I was eating, or standing outside, watching the boys run around, I thought of the future. They would be older, there'd be more money, and I'd be free, to do something I still hadn't identified.

One afternoon I went to the workshop to drop off some finished pairs. It was the same as usual in there, the radio on. Around the corner I saw the cracked feet of old Kadam, who always took a nap after lunch.

Pawar! said a short fellow near the door.

And, I said. What's happening? Borkar is a little younger than I but he was already bald. He looks foolish, which offsets the sly cast to his eyes; he resembles a slightly cunning baby.

We never see you, he said.

I'm there to be seen, I said, but suddenly I wasn't so sure.

Come out some evening, he said.

Out? I said.

Satpute sat a couple of places from Borkar. He had hair then, sparse but crow-black, a wizened face. He was thin, except for a slackness at the stomach, a weak but enduring sort of man. He put down his needle and made a tipping gesture towards his mouth.

Oh, I said. The truth is, I was at a loose end. I hadn't thought of myself as having spare time, before my affair with Ratna. My world had been hermetic: family and work. But I'd made time for those excursions, and now the seal was broken. I felt a little expectant all the time, a little disappointed. Maybe, I said. When?

Tonight, Satpute said.

Tonight, Borkar agreed. At sunset. We'll meet here.

There is a sort of chowk, outside the workshop, before the area where most of these people live. Our house is off the main road, a little separate.

Sunset? I said. We normally ate soon afterwards.

They nodded.

In the evening I told my wife I'd be going out.

Now? she said.

I have work, I said. You all go ahead and eat. I'll eat later. I left. I was annoyed with her for making me feel awkward. Had I no freedom? I shrugged it off and got to the workshop.

There was no one here, but a pale pi dog outside. I loitered next to the dog. Pages of an old calendar blew about. It was dusk; summer, and still very warm.

After a time, feeling let down, I squatted near the dog. I was hungry. I'd go back soon. I imagined our room, as though looking in, saw under the electric light my sons sitting down, my wife giving them rice and daal, and maybe some mutton. What was I doing here? I'd had my excitement. I couldn't expect life to go on in that way, waiting for a new surprise all the time, like a child.

The dog sighed, and began licking his balls. I got up.

Borkar and Satpute sidled down the road. Where have you been? I wanted to ask, but I'd lost confidence.

Come, Satpute said. We'll go to the bottle shop. You have money?

Obviously, I said. I felt the notes in my pocket.

Twenty minutes later, we were near the old godown. There were no lights here under the tree, near the tiny Datta temple. The air smelled like fields. I heard crickets.

Borkar had a bag. He took out three tumblers. The first bottle was opened. I'd drunk alcohol as a young man, but only a taste; I hadn't enjoyed it. I swigged as much as the others, and my stomach began to burn. The orange flavour was intense, like cheap perfume. I thought of Ratna and felt nostalgic.

Borkar said, This is better than sitting at home.

Satpute agreed. I looked at his drawn, yellow face, missed

my dinner, and said to myself, I am just seeing what this is like, I won't do it regularly.

A warm breeze sighed in the leaves of the banyan tree, and tickled my neck. Perhaps I'd spent too much time alone.

What are you chewing over? Borkar asked. There was an insensitivity about him, a humanity too, a warmth. I made these assessments as my father would have; my father who had always been, as far as I knew, so upright.

It's new to me to be among other men, I said. Not since I was younger, before I was married probably.

Don't you get bored at home? Satpute asked.

Bored, I said. I don't know. I felt the urge to defend my family. And was it boredom, or fear, the fear of being responsible, day after day, but with no idea how to go about things?

Leave him alone, Borkar said. He waved a fat paw at me.

There's no need to be uncomfortable, Satpute said. His smile showed browning teeth.

What about that woman of yours? Borkar asked.

I started, but it was Satpute who shrugged. It's going on, he said. Sometimes.

He too? The remaining light was orange, that orange dusk. Bats wheeled about the godown and the tree.

It's eerie here, I said, a little ghostly. This light.

They laughed. Pawar is a sensitive soul, Satpute said.

I laughed too, uneasily. A friend of my grandfather told us

a story when I was younger, I said. A man was walking home along a dark road near a forest.

Where was this? Satpute interrupted.

Bengal, I said, plucking the name out of the air.

Bengal? How would you know a story from Bengal?

I drank some more. Are you going to let me tell the story or not? I said.

He gave a dry laugh. Tell, tell, he said.

He had no light and was afraid of ghosts. But a fellow traveller with a lantern came along and kept him company. The first man was relieved.

Of course, Borkar said.

Satpute laughed. Were you there too, in Bengal?

Satpute, don't be an idiot. Who wants to walk alone near a forest?

I said, The two men talked and got to know each other. After a while the first man told the man with the lantern that when they met on the road he'd been afraid in case the other man was a ghost.

Oho! said Borkar, pouring more santra for all of us. I took my tumbler and put it against my foot so I'd know where it was. The sky was nearly dark. Even the bats were hardly visible, cinders against the darkness. It was silent. The city lights were far away. I thought of the field temple I used to walk to as a boy, its blunt found idols of Narsoba and his wives. I must be tipsy. The physical world slid away at an oblique angle.

Then what happened? Satpute said. He was a rough voice now, a few feet away in the dark.

Oh. Then the first man said he remembered it was all right because ghosts who take human form have feet that point backwards.

Ah, of course, said Borkar, as though this was well known.

I paused. Then the man carrying the lantern laughed, pointed it at his feet, and disappeared, I said.

Ah! So he was a ghost, Borkar said.

What do you think? I said. In the silence, I heard the crickets.

We should have had boiled peanuts, Satpute said. Something.

I was hungry too. Next time I'll bring something savoury, I said. My wife makes good chivda.

Chivda! We should have meat. Kebabs.

A confusion of acid moved in my stomach. My head began to float.

At first I enjoyed the uselessness of those evenings. We were like children, smutty children, it's true, but there was an innocence to it. I enjoyed being drunk, I discovered, the way things would suddenly loom closer, then swim back. It was like the way you get to know someone, like getting to know Ratna: those overwhelming moments of too much proximity, followed by retreating into distance.

*

Chaturthi was on a Sunday. After we took the children to the temple to see the idol, the rest of our stay was quiet. Mukta bai came in the mornings to cook. The house smelled of phenyl for hours after she'd cleaned. At lunch my wife would make bhakris. Then she'd watch television, and I'd rest. I'm not used to sleeping in the afternoon, but in the city it's possible to feel tired without doing much.

Two days before we were to leave I lay on Sohan's bed and felt myself slipping into unconsciousness. I stayed there a long time, it seemed, on the boundary between two states. Here in this house, and in my near-dream, the furniture of my life fell away. My things at home – the cupboard, the bed, Tuka with his orange fur and green eyes, the cracked bucket – seemed to be part of a dream. Like scraps of leather, oddly shaped, things from life, sayings, objects, found themselves spliced together. My father, walking past me, holding one chappal. My brother, stolid next to me outside the old house. In the dream he and I were talking about his daughter, whom he wants to marry off this winter. She's seventeen, a bright, calm girl.

Eventually I got up and went to the kitchen for tea.

We'll take a walk, she said, before the boys come home? I want to make sabudana vada for them.

Groggy, I sat at the table, reassembling the world, which wasn't mine. Tablecloth with pictures of fruit, ceiling fan, salt shaker. Photographs on a board behind the table. Pictures of the children, round-faced, Rohan serious, Sohan smiling.

None of it real. Did I have to go? Yes – no, I wasn't sure. Perhaps not yet.

We walked up the lane and turned right. We looked different from the other people around, she in her nine-yard sari, and I in my shirt and wide pyjamas. Or perhaps it wasn't what we were wearing. There aren't many people of our age in this area, and few people around in the daytime. Everyone's working or at school. She smiled at a watchman we've passed before, and a man selling sukha bhel.

How do you know all these people when we've just been here a few days? I grumbled.

I don't walk around pretending the world doesn't exist, she said.

Sometimes I think I'm the one who doesn't exist, I said. My penis twinged. Could I need to go again?

Oh, you exist, she said drily.

Sanjay wants to marry off Sangita, I said. He should let her study a bit longer, let her work.

But you knew this. What do you think she should work as?

Something. She could move to the city. She might want to train, work in a beauty parlour, she said. What's the point of just getting her married? I said. Half my mind was on my dream, half on the probably misleading urgency I was experiencing.

A koel screeched in a tree as we passed.

Quiet! I said.

She began to laugh.

The koel screamed louder and louder.

These city birds are deranged, I said.

You don't think she should be married? she said.

What's the hurry? I said. Of course she should. But why now? She'll just become an accessory to her husband's life. What's the value of that?

I was sure now. I did need to go. Let's go back, I said.

She stopped. It seemed to me suddenly that she was trembling. But I don't want to go back yet, she said.

Come on, I urged. I need to get back. Don't delay.

She stood irresolute.

Or take your time, if you want, I said. Give me the key. I hurried back, past the screaming koels. When I got to the bathroom, I leaked a few hot drops. She had come back too, but when I went to the kitchen where she was frying the vade, she didn't look at me.

I keep thinking about death, as though death were the answer to life, an answer that removed the uncertainty. But maybe simply to be answered is consoling. She knows this, and when she is angriest with me she says nothing. The timing is confusing. It's not straight after I've done something I shouldn't. For example, nothing happened immediately after the episode with Ratna. Though my wife didn't, I think, know about it, but she might have, for superstitiously I find it hard to believe she doesn't know everything I do and think. And then, at times, when I realise I can pass unnoticed, get away with things, I become callous and think I don't need her approval. That's when she stops paying me attention, and I suffocate. It's not that she stops talking, or stops cooking, nothing obvious. She doesn't sound angry or depressed. I just stop existing.

It's a living death. She is still there, but the invisible current that irritates me, the thread between me and her, is not only gone but it's as though it never had been.

The first time it happened, after Ratna, I watched myself, as though I were my own ghost; I pitied my lumpy existence as I shambled from my room to the kitchen. This poor fool, this clod of matter. He had just enough spark of consciousness to suffer from the hostility of everything that was not him.

Even now, I did whatever I could to annoy her, to get a reaction. I made a noise when getting up at night. I banged the bathroom door. I dropped the soap. I talked to myself.

What's the matter? I said loudly the next afternoon. We were sitting silently in front of the television. The news was on, and a reporter was talking about the rape of that child, in Kolhapur. There'd been an outcry, and the police said they had a suspect.

Why are you watching this? I said. It's depressing. I turned off the television.

She looked at me without anger.

What's the matter? I approached, put my face close to hers, felt her forehead. You seem ill, I'm worried about you! I said. I peered into her face. What's wrong?

After we had been home a day she relented. I knew it wasn't because of my manoeuvres. I didn't care. All that mattered was that she relented. It's not that she is unable to maintain her solitude, or that she gets angry – that would be a victory.

I think what happens is that her belief in her rightness wavers. She isn't sure whether she should, after all, feel sorry for me. Her compunction, her being a good person, or is it her weakness, I don't care, it gives her doubt, it creates a chink. After all, I see her consider, the fair part of her, which is enormous, which has shaped all our lives, after all, perhaps I should come back. Perhaps he needs me.

In this way she never gets whatever it is that she needs; she is always brought back to earth, to the ugly world of truck horns and the cracked plastic bucket; the groove in the latrine floor that never looks clean; to our pots and pans that are blackened and wearing out; to my inadequacies, which never come to a final crisis, but simply limp on. I do it to her every time. And then I breathe again, and am comforted, and insensitive, as before.

4

All in the head

Shouldn't you meet the doctor? she said.

I pretended not to hear.

About your problem, she went on.

I raised my head. I'd just sat down, after going out to check whether I needed to go and finding, no, not really. It's not as bad when I'm working. Perhaps it's all in the head after all, the problems of my cock. I looked vaguely at her and went back to sewing on a belt.

There's a new doctor in the clinic, she said the next evening, the clinic near the workshop.

Oh?

Yes. He sees patients after five.

I felt a shiver of anxiety, down there. I'd gone to see the doctor once before, when I stopped drinking. All kinds of health problems began then. My back started to hurt; one knee became weak. My stomach roared with acidity. The doctor was a young man, new to the practice and the area. He didn't last. He told me the drinking had caused the problems. I said more likely it was the stopping. Still, something told me it might be an idea to take a break.

That was the start of old age. Perhaps I was merely accepting the inevitable.

What was the point of doctors? I had to pay him so that he'd tell me I was getting older, I should eat on time, take exercise, and so forth. Things anyone knows.

On Sunday I heard my wife saying to Prakash, Talk to him. He should see someone, about his problem.

I don't have a problem! I shouted from the inside room, startling my grandson. I'm going out, I said.

But Anil is here, said my wife's voice behind me. It was no use. In the moment of losing my temper I saw the next step, which was to walk out. I took it. Even as I began to march off in the direction of my usual walk I thought that it would have been possible to react otherwise. But I hadn't. I felt defeated, and irritated. It was too hot for all this, and I'd eaten well at lunch. I carried on walking, and salty sweat ran in a line down my neck.

I found myself going towards the workshop. That same dusty lane, and a page of a newspaper blowing outside it. I turned in a different direction, into back streets. Before long I was passing Ratna's house. How treacherous of my feet to lead me here. I hadn't thought of her in a long time. The door was a different colour. Was it the same one? Yes. A child came out, and stared at me. I resumed walking. The things your family drives you to. If they could only let me be as I was, we would all get along. And if they fixed the small things they ought. My wife has few flaws, but it's exhausting to live with someone who's always right, someone who's so self-sufficient. Since the time we were first married, she's kept things to herself, what things I wouldn't know, but there's been a part of her that wasn't available to me. She liked to spend time alone. Everyone in the house used to comment on it. She'd go to wash clothes, and would be some time returning. I wondered if she had a friend she talked to, or even a man she was meeting.

One day my sister-in-law told us all, laughing, that she'd seen my wife sitting under a tree near the river, just staring. It became a joke.

What do you do, when you go off? I asked her, and she only smiled, or waved a hand, as though she wasn't to be questioned.

Over time you get used to the unknown areas of the person you live with. They become familiar, or that's what you think.

I seemed to have brought my wife on this walk. I turned, no longer angry, and began to go home. I saw things: a hoarding for a new film with Akshay Kumar, a myna sitting on top of a wall, chattering, looking at me with friendly brown eyes; the carcass of a crow on the road, worms coming out of it. I would forgive my family, I decided, despite their lack of respect and their annoying behaviour. Also, it was time to get home in case I needed to piss. I walked a little faster, and passed the market, and the office with the black glass window, the white lettering, Dr Nitin Sonawane.

They had to leave, my wife said when I returned.

But they hardly got here, I said. Did you all have tea?

There's some in the pan, she said.

*

That night, returned from the outhouse, I said into the darkness, It's true, it is bothering me. I settled heavily on to the bed. I'm so tired, I said.

The silence was attentive.

You want me to say you're right, is that it? I said. I feel very cranky, I added after a pause, perhaps unnecessarily. I sighed loudly. The weight of the world, existence, etc.

What will a doctor do anyway? I said.

The silence had a quality. It wasn't sullen, or expectant.

I said, I could go and see him, I suppose.

She turned on her side, towards me.

Who knows, I said. I may drop in to see him one evening.

A bony, warm hand patted my arm.

I rolled over too, away from her. How strange our conversations could be. I like to talk things through. I need comfort. She can be like an animal in its shell, perfectly content. You see her drinking her tea, or listening to the radio while she cooks, reading the newspaper or watching a serial, and there's nothing missing. It's not that I want her to be unhappy, but for someone like me, always teetering from one desire to the next, it's hard to be around her. Yet it's to her that I return when I've tired myself out.

She turned over again and so did I, our slow synchronised dance in the bed.

She told me about her childhood only after we'd been married some time – after we moved into the new house. I should have been happy. For a while I was. Then I was discontented. I didn't know what to do with myself. Prakash was already on the way. I was used to being crammed into the old house, used to being able to be forgotten.

I would get angry about nothing. You make yourself unhappy, she said. Well, I said, if we relied on you where would we be? You think everyone is nice, wanting to help you. We'd probably be cheated, lose our livelihood. Someone has to be a grown-up.

As I shouted I wanted, I remember, to weep at the idea of having to be a grown-up.

It was after that argument that she sat down and sighed. No, she said, it wasn't easy for her. She told me things I'd half known – that she'd grown up at first living with her grandmother, in Bhimashankar. I thought she was my mother, she said. Then when I was seven I had to go back. My father came for me. I didn't know who he was. I cried and cried. I was back in the city, living with everyone else, and there was no space. The air didn't smell the way it did at home. My mother – wasn't good to me.

She shrugged.

My mother – I began.

But she went on and I thought with resentment, Oh, now I have to listen to her.

I waited every day for the time when I'd be able to go back to my grandparents. But both of them died before I could visit. I wasn't taken to the ceremonies. I wanted to die. I was such a young child, but I thought about it all the time, death, and when it would come, so I could be with my grandmother again, in the forest where the air smelled different and there were a hundred things to see every hour, and I was free.

Her eyes clouded. Her face looked as I had never seen it – inward, bitter. I was thrilled, yet repelled. The moments when I understood her best, accepted her as she was, were also the moments when I was absolutely without desire for her. As though in being a person it was impossible for me also to be a man.

For a while I was like that, very unhappy, she said.

And then things improved, I said quickly.

She smiled at me, her lopsided smile. There was a neighbour near my parents' house who took an interest in children, she said. Particularly me. He used to call me to his house when his wife wasn't there.

What?

She was shaking slightly. I didn't tell anyone, she said.

What did he do?

She shook her head. It wasn't that bad, but it was enough.

Did he –?

No, she said, and I was ashamed, because I was thinking of myself, and what someone might have done to my wife before I knew her.

A tear rolled down her face. She said, I couldn't tell anyone. But then he did it to someone else, and he got beaten up and had to move. My mother told me if anything had happened to me it was my fault.

I took her hand then, and she let me. I was crying too. I didn't know what I felt.

She took away her hand, and wiped her face. The baby in her was starting to show.

And then, she said, I decided that I would never be unhappy again; that I would expect nothing from life, but just enjoy whatever I could – a cool breeze, clean clothes, walking to school, or being alone. If bad things happened, I knew they would pass. I knew I would live a long life. But I also knew I couldn't depend on anyone or anything to be happy. She looked at me again, and her eyes were clear and warning. It's a choice, she said.

But still, I argued with her now, as she slept next to me, it's easier for you. You don't need people. And everyone loves you. Whereas I …

When I woke it was bright. I was late for the start of the day.

*

Outside, said the girl at the counter.

But I want to see the doctor, I said. An older man with white hair, spectacles, a stick, looked at me. He was sitting on one of the three chairs inside the door.

Chappals.

Oh, I said.

I went to the door, removed them, came back, and helped her fill in a form about me. A pert young thing, dark-skinned, in a pink kurta and dupatta, with shiny pink nails.

She pointed to the chairs. I sat a little away from the older man. Perhaps he was in his seventies or eighties. The future, I thought. He looked fine, apart from the cane and the thick spectacles.

In the afternoon, she'd asked me, Shall I come with you? No no, I said, though I wanted her to.

Arun Pawar, said the thin figure in the office door.

I padded in.

Please sit. He closed the door behind me and retreated behind the desk, on which there was a computer, a calendar, pens, little statues.

And what's the matter? he said.

My wife thought I should see you, I said. There's nothing wrong with me.

What are the symptoms?

I looked over at the high bed. Well, I said, basically nothing. Some, ah, irregularities when I piss.

He nodded, waving his long hands. Your age?

Sixty-seven.

How long has this been going on?

Not long. A few months. Maybe a year. It bothers me at night, I said. I wake up, then I can't go back to sleep.

How's the stream?

What stream?

When you urinate. Is it weak?

I had a sense I should save being irritated for later.

Sometimes, I said.

When you've urinated, do you find your bladder is empty?

No.

The stream starts and stops? He kept writing.

Yes, I said. I rubbed my forehead.

This happens often?

Yes.

He nodded. His face was smooth, oddly comical.

You're fully qualified? I found myself asking.

My certificates.

I peered behind him at a row of framed documents. Sorry, I said.

I'm going to check your prostate.

My what?

Just a minute. He got up, took down a large book and

began leafing through it until he got to the diagram of a man's lower half, all kinds of pink tubes inside the body. This is your bladder, he said. This is your prostate. Its function is to do with helping the semen come out when you ejaculate.

He looked into my eyes. His were large and brown, framed by oblong wire spectacles. But after the age of fifty, he went on, this tends to enlarge. Most of the time that doesn't mean something bad.

And the rest of the time?

First let me explain. So this – finger circling one of the pink things – is your prostate. It's normally the size of a bor. But when it becomes enlarged, it presses here on your bladder. Which could be causing these difficulties regarding your urination.

I nodded quickly.

Now I just need to examine you, he said. There's nothing to be alarmed about.

Examine my –?

Come to the bed here. Take down your trousers and bend over. Put your hands here. I'm –

I heard the sound of rubber being stretched. I whipped around, pulling my neck. Agh! I said.

He was putting on a rubber glove. It'll only take a short time, he said. Bend over and try to relax.

No, I thought. Pull up your clothes and run. But I felt myself bending, and holding the end of the rickety bed.

You have to relax, he said.

The insistent finger probed. Thank God I was usually regular in the morning. Otherwise – But to my shame, the air began to smell as you would expect, if one person were poking around in another's bottom. The thought gave me an adolescent giggle. I relaxed, and the finger shot up further, and probed in areas I wasn't even aware of, rotated. There was a tingling behind my belly button; even at the base of my penis.

I moaned very quietly, feeling myself lose control of everything.

That's it, he said, and suddenly I was uncorked. The smell persisted.

You can dress, he said. He walked past me, to a small steel sink where he stripped off the gloves and washed his hands many times. Please sit, he said, over his shoulder.

When we were face to face again I smiled bashfully, hoping he'd make a sign the encounter hadn't horrified him. He didn't. Well, he said, your prostate is a little enlarged. It isn't hardened, which is good. We'll do a blood test to get more information. He scribbled on a sheet of paper. Take this to the lab around the corner. The receptionist will give you directions. Collect the report, bring it back to me, and then we'll know the next step.

I blinked. So you don't know what it is? There's nothing to be done?

We need to see what the blood test says.

What are the treatments? My voice sounded querulous, wavering.

He looked down. It really depends on what the problem is, and how much it affects you. There are medicines that could give relief. Surgery is possible, though usually that's only if the symptoms are really making a patient's life difficult.

It's expensive?

It's expensive, and has varying results.

So there's nothing to be done?

Let me know when you have the test results, he said. He stood, and I collected myself, and the piece of paper.

When I got home I was still thinking about the lab, and watching a red line climb into a syringe, along a thin pipe, into a clear container. It had been a bad day for my body. Well, I began as I got in the door, that was an experience.

Sayali called, she said. Prakash has been arrested.

Oh for God's sake, I said. What?

There was that demonstration, about the child's rape. Sayali wasn't sure what to do. Will you find out?

But what happened?

Maybe some sort of fight.

But that would have been expected, I said. I'd forgotten, there was to be a demonstration of sorts against north Indians, because the suspected rapist was a north Indian. Normally Prakash isn't political, but neither are these demonstrations. Just some men drinking, shouting slogans, and maybe hitting some other men. The police let it go on.

Sayali has to stay home, to look after Anil, my wife said.

I'm going, I'm going, I said ill-temperedly.

At the station there was a knot of people. What happened? I said.

A man told me, A few people got into a scuffle at the demonstration. One of them hit a police officer. Then the police got angry and took three of them in.

I'm looking for my son, I said. I named him.

The other man glanced at me. I'm waiting for my brother, he said. Pawar, I think that was one of the names. Prakash Arun Pawar?

Yes. But he wouldn't have hit a policeman.

Three hours later my son emerged, his eyes red, his clothing crumpled. His face was puffy.

Let's go, he said briefly. They'll be wondering where I am at home.

They are wondering, I said. I heard my voice rise. What happened?

Not here, he said. He began to walk off. He looked back. Oh, he said. All right. We'll get a ride. Do you have money?

In the rickshaw he said, I wasn't charged yet. Just … and he felt the right side of his face, which was darker and larger than usual. He sighed and leaned back. He smelled of stale booze.

You hit a policeman?

There was a lafda, he said. I felt someone grab me from behind and I stuck out my elbow. I think I caught him in the face. Then we got taken in.

You're wasting your life, I said. It just came out.

He looked at me sideways. You'd know, he said. He stuck his tongue experimentally into a corner of his right cheek, and closed his eyes. His fingers, the nails unclean, travelled carefully over the side of his face.

I became very angry and said nothing. What a day I'd had.

At home I got out of the rickshaw, gave the driver some money and went inside.

Well? she said. Has he gone?

Your son is fine, I said. But he's an idiot. He'll get home in a few minutes. I hobbled towards the outhouse.

The next morning, I was stitching. Prakash's remark still rankled. Let it go, I told myself. I had no authority. I hadn't been much of a father to them. Especially Deepak. He'd borne the worst of the drinking – Prakash was married and moved out towards the end of it. The enormity of having children, being responsible, bringing them up into men, it had been too much. I'd sought distraction. After the fact, when they were married and older, I was remorseful. I wanted them to say I'd done a good job, that things were all right.

It didn't happen. They remained closer to their mother. They rarely told me things. I couldn't understand it. I'd treated them as equals. Perhaps that was the mistake. My father always maintained his dignity. If he had crises, I never saw them. Was it because of the way I'd been – the things I'd done? Not that they knew all of them.

As I pulled the leather thread, made another hole with the hook and threaded it through again, I was thinking about Ratna. All that time ago – fifteen years. More than my eldest grandson's life. When I walked by her house, or the one I think it was, I felt time hadn't passed at all. I could have gone in, pushed open the door as I did that first afternoon, on an errand to collect some hides because the delivery man, her husband, was new.

5

The hides

Her eyes were suspicious and amused. They were large, but not particularly beautiful: very dark, really black. Her complexion was dark too. There was a strong smell about her. Now I wonder if I remember this from that first time, or if I added it from what I knew later. It was the smell of sex, the way she smelled between her legs.

I explained what I needed, that a messenger from the shop had told me to collect some hides.

She opened the door. The back, she said. Shut the door.

I did so, and followed her ample hips as they swayed inside. The house was dark, boxes here and there. They hadn't lived there long. It was damp; the rains were going on.

At the back of the room was another door. She went through it and I followed. This room was dark too; the door to the yard was shut. She indicated the corner and I, unable to see, went towards it. There was a mattress and I thought perhaps the hides were piled next to it, though I didn't see them. I turned. She was quite close to me, smelling strongly. Suddenly her hand was on my crotch, where something happened. It was as though, there in the dark, under the knowing gaze of a woman who seemed to know what I wanted before it had occurred to me, I became unable to think in words. She opened my trousers and her rough hand held me, arousal so extreme it was nearly painful.

Don't undress, she said. She pulled me down, sat on the mattress and pulled up her sari and petticoat. I remember looking up at the window, which had been covered with an old atta sack. She took my hand and put it between her legs. She was already moist, and I smelled her – she smelled of sweat, and animal.

She licked the end of my penis, and again painful things happened. Then she pulled at my hips and helped me inside. She was wet and muscular. She hooked her legs around my back, showed me the rhythm she wanted, and unfastened her blouse. Her breasts were round, not too drooping. I squeezed as hard as I wanted. I think I banged my head against the cupboard that stood behind the mattress. Soon, I felt a stronger gripping, and her breathing changed. I exploded, and lay quivering on top of her. A few seconds later, I wondered what I was doing.

I jumped up and pulled up my trousers.

She sat, looking slightly irritated, and wiped herself with

her petticoat. Over there, she said. The hides were stacked near the door leading to the outer room. Somehow I hadn't seen or smelled them. The entire room smelled of her, I mean of her cunt.

I picked up the hides and felt my ankle wobble.

Not tomorrow, she said, but the day after is fine. This sort of time. She sounded bored, like a housewife talking to a visiting workman. I said nothing and stumbled out. The rain had abated into a drizzle. There were rivulets in the narrow gullies as I walked out of the neighbourhood and back towards the main road. As I walked my clothes and hair and the hides I was carrying became damp. I reached home, said that the new delivery man hadn't been there, that things seemed disorganised, that I'd got wet and felt a little tired. I would lie down for a minute. I got under the blanket and slept blissfully. When I woke, my mind was clear and my body light. My son returned from school. My other son was at work. My wife started cooking. The rain became heavier. Our house smelled of food, and rain, and leather. The electric bulb was put on, for it was too dark to see. I worked, cutting out soles, very calm and happy. It was out of the question to think of what had happened, or consider it a mistake. As well as the lightness in my balls, and the extreme peace, relaxation and wellbeing in my body, I had the feeling I had floated above everything – the factory line of my existence, of making chappals and feeding my children, of looking at my wife and failing to feel united with her, failing to feel that I belonged in my life. Other than this sudden sense of liberation, which it seemed no one around could perceive in me, there was nothing to say that those few minutes of the afternoon had even taken place. No one would know, and the incident of course would not be repeated. But it had happened.

III

Shoes

21

His good white shirt

It's Granddad, I told Jason. He's dead. Heart attack. Alison phoned me.

Was it on my birthday? His voice sounded raw.

No, the day after.

Did it take a long time?

No. He had a heart attack in the night and died just after he got to the hospital, she said. The funeral's the day after tomorrow. They thought it'd take longer to organise. Do you want to come back?

Long silence. On the other end of the phone I heard sunshine and beer and girls and sand. I told him he should do whatever seemed best, and it'd be all right.

You're going, though, aren't you?

I'll go, I said.

Alison had said she wasn't sure there'd be room for me

in the first car, with family. What with her, and Paul, and Mum, and the kids. Don't worry about that, I said. I'll take a taxi. Knowing she probably wanted to annoy me didn't make me less angry. I saw myself walking in, standing at the back, leaving without anyone knowing.

In the end Jason said he'd come back. He got a ticket, but texted to say the train was late getting to London. Alison called right after. She said they'd been thinking (not Mum, not her, they) that it wouldn't look nice if I arrived alone, so would I come to the house at 9.45 sharp to take the car with them? The kids were going to a neighbour's house till afterwards. Was Jason coming? I said he was delayed, but on the way. He'd meet us there.

In the car, I sat in near silence. Mum was crying, angrily, and Alison was snivelling. Paul looked distracted, like the rugby was on somewhere. Through the tinted windows I stared at the things we passed. That pub that was always changing landlords and breweries, the Swan. The shop near our house, it used to be called Goblin. Now it was a Londis.

The drive was long. Mum had had her hair set. She looked old, and my first reaction was she'd done it on purpose. At some point I'd stopped noticing them getting older. They'd stuck in my head at forty-five or fifty, and when I saw them afterwards I felt surprised, then put out, as though they were trying to get my sympathy with their wrinkles and their white hair.

Alison had had her hair done too. When did Paul get so

fat? His white shirt looked used, like it was his good white shirt. Alison's outfit seemed new. Sweetheart neckline. I was wearing a black pencil dress and I liked my shoes. I'd got them in the factory shop a while ago. T-bars, with a conical heel. Viviana, if I remember correctly. Well, it's not every day you go to your dad's funeral, is it? What I really wanted to ask was if the casket was closed, but there was no one I felt I could ask.

The atmosphere at the crematorium was like a weird film premiere. A crowd was waiting outside, and we pulled up after the hearse and got out, very slowly, not really looking at anyone. I felt curious eyes on me. We filed into the small chapel and sat in the front row. Celebrities.

I couldn't concentrate. I kept thinking how funny Dad would have found it – he hates churches. The priest talked about bringing him home to God. I thought about the body in the coffin, wearing a suit no doubt. Shoes on his dead feet. That must have been an operation. How many funerals must happen a day, and the schedule, and how they didn't let you in till it was time for your slot, like the cinema. Did any-one try and sneak a double bill? I thought about everything, except Dad. And I waited for my son to arrive, kicking open the back doors like a cowboy, firing his silver pistol into the ceiling. It didn't happen. Before long I was following the others as we touched the foot of the coffin, peeped into it. They'd put his glasses on. What was in there had nothing to do with my dad. I kept expecting to see him outside, with a joke and a plan. Then we went out, and walked to the grave. I threw a bit of earth on the coffin along with the rest, and that's when I started crying.

22

A bottle of something

In the chapel I'd caught a glimpse of Neil, Uncle Neil. At the house he was standing in the front room, in his shiny suit. I walked in and felt like turning around and leaving. But I didn't want to go in the kitchen: my mum and Alison were there and some other women, doing helpful things with the sandwiches and talking about it being a mercy in the end, or something. I got distracted, remembering that when I'd been little I used to love being with my mum. I'd follow her from room to room till she turned and shouted, For heaven's sake!

Kind of fucked up if you think about it, which I didn't want to. You're thirty-five, I reminded myself. Your son's sixteen. Going on seventeen. A song.

Suddenly I was in the middle of a hug from Neil. Oh Je— I said, into his double-breasted jacket. He smelled of Superkings and sweat.

I know, he said. I know. You poor little girl. I got crushed again in polyester and squirmed till he let go. Anyone else would have been embarrassed. He looked happy. There were tears on his face. Did you see him? he asked.

I didn't even think about whether he meant dead or alive. I said what I'd been planning to say from the time I left home that morning: I don't want to talk about it.

You should talk, let it all out.

I stretched my mouth at him and backed into a corner of the room. Uncle Andy shambled in, and so did Alison with a huge tray of sandwiches. We borrowed six trays, she said. You never think, do you? About things like trays.

I wondered when I could smoke.

When Jason got there I felt less strange. He looked taller, browner. There were shadows under his eyes, and he wasn't drinking. Hangover, eh? I said. He rolled his eyes. He was swept into a wave of women: my mother, Alison, other people. All talking shit. He was wearing the suit he bought last year in a charity shop. That boy knows how to dress when he wants to. All of a sudden I wanted to lay my head against something, the side of the sofa, plush velvet, not the one we used to have but one like it, and close my eyes. I stayed sitting up, sipping some horrible wine.

After a while he sat next to me. Mum, can I go out and smoke?

Let's go, I said.

Is that all right?

Well, what are we waiting for? I said. As though if we sat there long enough Dad would walk in. Everything would be normal. I'd lost track of what that was.

I went up to Mum. We're off now, I said. I'll come and see you. I'll ring you before.

Alison looked disbelieving.

See you soon, Jason said to them. He squeezed Mum's shoulder. Bye, Auntie Alison. He's good at things like this. He manages to seem warm, without committing to anything. They all say he's a lovely boy.

We walked home slowly. The afternoon was warm. The sun and the early start and not having eaten made me feel lightheaded. The hot pavement and the smells of petrol in the air and grass in the verges put me back in a summer twenty years ago, or more. Eating an ice lolly shaped like a spaceship sat on the parapet outside the shop, with Katie, both of us swinging our legs and frowning into the sun. The whole summer ahead of us, nothing to do except work and go out and think about boys.

Are you all right, Mum? said the boy next to me. He could have been a friend from long ago, and he looked suspiciously like the first boy I'd fallen in love with, but that part of my life was gone. I was too tired to put everything in order. Just the summer, and petrol, grass, hot air, the smell of disappointment, a disappointment you couldn't explain.

That was horrible, wasn't it? I said. He lit a cigarette, gave it to me, lit another for himself.

Let's get ice cream on the way home, I said. Let's sit in the garden. And let's get a bottle of something.

He nodded.

When we were in the garden, him in his shorts, me in a really old summer dress, faded from blue to a washing-powder colour, and us halfway through a bottle of Cava that we'd bought in the Spar because it seemed like a special occasion moment and I quite fancied it, Jason said, Mum.

Yes, I said after a bit. I had my knackered straw hat over the top of my face and I was lying on my back on the rug.

I want to ask you some stuff about my dad.

Oh, I said.

I've been thinking about him, he said.

Right. I tried sitting up, and rolled on to my side instead. The light was bright behind Jason's head. His voice was low and hummed with, something. Maybe he was worried I'd get angry.

What do you want to know? I said. You know I haven't heard from him.

I know. That's not it.

I waited. I sat up again and looked in my glass. I poured us both some more wine.

Jason crossed his feet at the ankles. He held one ankle with his hand. He looked up at me. Tell me about him, he said. What was he like?

What was he like?

He nodded and cleared his throat. Yeah, he said.

I don't know what order to tell you, I said.

Tell me as you think of it. What was he like when you first knew each other?

I was just thinking about that, I said. I laughed. You know, for years in my mind he was a man. We were young, but he was the first man I was with, the first man I loved. You know.

A nod.

And now, I said, it's so strange, because even though he was about your age when we – when I first knew him, he seems so much younger. And I do. Than you. I don't know if it's because I'm looking back, or we were just younger then, younger than people your age are now. Or what.

I put the hat on my head. The first thing I thought of when you asked what he was like was his bedroom, I said.

Jason looked appalled. I laughed. Not like that. But it was exactly like him. There was a mattress on the floor. A tape player. A desk. His portfolio case, with his drawings. There'd be tapes on the floor, and his sketchbook. And a hoodie on the back of the chair. His tobacco on the floor near the bed. A lamp. You know he smoked rollies, it wasn't that cool to smoke rollies then.

He nodded.

Did I ever tell you the kinds of things he used to draw?

No.

Well, he had to draw stuff for his course. Art foundation. Buildings, portraits, studies, still lifes. But when he was at home listening to music he'd draw two things over and over.

One was these drawings that were like dreams, and in them there'd be girls with long hair, and trees, and houses, and animals, but not animals you could recognise, all kind of melted into each other. I used to ask him what they were and once he said they're maps of dreams. Maps of dreams. I loved being around someone who'd talk like that. It wasn't exactly normal.

Grin from Jason; no comment. I wondered if he was pegging his mother as the kind of girl who fell for this sort of thing – bad drawings of unicorns and a bit of floaty music.

The other thing he used to draw a lot, over and over, was this tree next to his window, I said. It was an old house, up near Mousehold. Sash windows. There was a tree outside – I think it was a horse chestnut. The branches hung past the window, that was the view from the bed and he'd draw it quickly most days, some days spend ages, do it in watercolour or acrylic or whatever. He had this series of drawings and paintings of the view from the window. Leaves of different colours. He used to say this thing, a quotation, he said, Claire, Picasso said painting is like keeping a diary. He loved that.

I was enjoying talking about it. It surprised me.

One of the reasons I think about his room is that it really reminds me of him, I said. The things that were special about him. He did things a different way from other people I knew. I started plaiting three blades of grass to make a rope, tore one, and dropped it. Like, he had a mattress on the floor instead of a bed. Or he didn't have much stuff. He could make something amazing out of very little.

I looked at my son. He was concentrating.

I think because they'd moved around so much, you know, the family, I went on. Because of his dad's job. He was good at being self-contained, Pete. I'd never known anyone like that. He was patient, as well. He could be on his own a lot. He didn't get bored. Um, what else? I asked myself. I saw Pete, around the first time he began to appear. I'd never really noticed him.

That's another thing, I said. He was good-looking, your dad. You look a lot like him. He was tall like you, same colouring, you know that. He was a little thinner. His hair was a bit long, not super-long. Not like long. Maybe just around here. I waved at my neck. He wore those flannel shirts a lot of people wore. I never really noticed him before I knew him, maybe because he was new. He was good at fitting in without being noticed.

I looked into my son's blue eyes.

And even though he was so good-looking, because he wasn't one of the boys that was considered fit, he just didn't really get noticed. It's funny how that happens in school.

Jason nodded. Yeah, he said.

You know, I said, I bet it wouldn't be that difficult to find him now. With the internet. Is that what you were thinking?

He cleared his throat. I've looked, he said. It's a common name.

Yeah. Peter Stephenson.

But someone – a friend of mine – helped me look, he said.

She found someone that might be him. I was going to write to that person and find out. There was a drawing, instead of a profile picture. It looked a bit like me. That's what she noticed.

I drank what was left in my glass. When was this? I said.

Only in the last couple of months, really.

I see.

But I didn't email him, Jason said. I don't want to, yet. When – when you realised you were pregnant with me, what did he say?

I thought about it. I can't really remember, Jason, I said. We were both really surprised, and then there was telling my parents. Everything became a nightmare. Nan said I could live with her. I can't remember what Pete said he was going to do. I think there was talk of him getting a job. His parents were going to move again in a few months. He said something about the army. And he was the least likely person you could think of to join the army, honestly. There was that shop then, the same one that's there now, the army recruiters.

And then?

There was all that stuff at home, I said. And at the same time your Uncle Jim was moving away. And I was moving into Nan's. My mother wasn't speaking to me, but she was speaking about me, a lot. It was like war had broken out. My dad didn't want me to leave, but he had nothing to say to her.

Jason nodded.

I moved the grass plait out of sight. Somewhere in the

middle of it, I said, I had the feeling that Pete might not be around that much longer. Everything changed when – it wasn't the same. We couldn't be on our own, we couldn't be us any more. I think he thought for a bit that he'd do something, make it better. But instead all this other stuff started happening. The grown-ups stepped in. His parents weren't happy. Didn't want him to ruin – didn't want him to change his plans.

Jason was pulling out blades of grass.

I breathed out. In a way, I said, I'm only putting this together now. I was so sad about it, forever. And so angry. I half believed a lot of what other people said. And Pete and I seemed so grown up. I couldn't believe he'd just go. Even though I had the feeling –

What? Jason said. His eyes met mine.

I had the feeling he wouldn't stay, I said. It's like with his room, the way he lived. He was good at being him, good at making something nice and fun and special out of wherever he was. But he also had this instinct not to weigh himself down. I thought for ages, told myself, if he'd loved me he would have stayed. If he left it's because he never loved me.

I looked at Jason for a second. His face was stony. I looked at next door's tree, a branch hanging over our wall, afternoon sun on a ruddy apple.

But now I don't know if I think that, I went on. It's like you. I look at you now and you're almost the same age. I can't imagine you with a baby and a girlfriend in a council flat, can you? I think he just knew it wasn't the right time, he wasn't ready. He probably thought it was for the best when he stopped keeping in touch, that we'd both be able to move on. I looked down at the grass marks on my feet.

But I wouldn't be like that, Jason said. If I – I wouldn't. I'd take responsibility.

I know, I said. You're different people. I don't think he did the best thing, but it was the best he could do. Jason!

What?

You're not – I mean you haven't – have you? Is there – do you? Is there a girl?

He grinned at me. No, Mum. I mean – no.

How do you mean?

Mum, he said. He picked up the bottle, poured some into my glass, emptied the rest into his and drank it. Don't worry, Mum, he said. You don't have to think about anything like that.

Jesus, I said. I hope not. That'd be the last –

I'd make a better job of it, though.

I laughed. You would, but – not now. God, I've got a headache.

My son got up, tall against the sun. I'm going to take a shower, he said.

Okay, I said. I watched him go into the house.

23

The way she is

We went on the same as before. Jason went to work, and out with his friends. He left his clothes in a mountain at the end of his bed. I went in to get them. I went to work. I walked home. I thought about Damian. It hadn't finished hurting but it had to take a rest. I couldn't think about it right now.

I phoned my mum, got Alison, and said I'd go round to see Mum on Friday after work. Alison said that'd be a good time because she, Alison, would be at work, and she didn't like leaving Mum alone too much, as it was a sensitive time.

Right, I said.

I thought about it, and about odd things like my bedroom, and how it used to be – the lampshade I'd painted, the rag rug, whether the hall smelled the same, whether I'd go in the back door or the front door, what to wear. In the end I nearly got late for work. The morning was mad busy, checking orders for three new-season shoes.

Walking along, I realised I'd forgotten the names of some of the roads. My feet knew the way, like in a dream. I kept putting my hand in my pocket as I walked, as though to see if I had my old back-door key.

Be calm, I told myself. There's nothing to lose now. When I stood outside the front door, which I'd never used when I lived there, and rang the doorbell, I felt strange and detached.

An old woman answered, and peered through the crack. Hello, she said suspiciously.

Mum, I said.

Ah, come in, she said. She opened the door wider and smiled a sort of smile. I gave her an awkward kiss on the cheek and followed her into the kitchen.

I'll put the kettle on, she said. When it was hissing she put a tin on the table. I made these yesterday, she said. You used to like them.

The tin was filled with chocolate cornflake cakes in little paper cases. Oh, I said. I still like them. I got one out and started to eat it: the same sticky crunch. I could have been ten years old, back from school.

She poured hot water in the mugs and spent a while harassing the tea bags with a spoon. Before I could say anything, she'd put sugar in one mug and given it to me. It was sweet – after all these years.

How are you? I asked.

She sat down slowly, with a sigh. People have been sending cards, she said.

I'd noticed them, some on the table, some on the side.

That's nice, I said, for something to say.

In the end though, she said, you're on your own, aren't you?

I sneaked a glance at her face, bitterness settled into its soft white folds. She's been preparing for this most of her life. In the end you're on your own, so I'll act now as if I'm on my own. I'll go around behaving as selfishly as possible and complaining about everyone else.

Hold on, I told myself. Stop it. Just stop. I stopped.

Alison's been very good, hasn't she? I said.

My mother made a face. She has, she said. Of course it's family you really want.

I blinked. Let's see, I said. How long have they been together now?

I knew how long. It was about the time I got pregnant. Paul is five years older than me, and Alison was his friend's girlfriend. Trevor dumped her, and Paul was there.

And how are you, Claire? she said. Her hands palms up on the table, face direct. Nothing to pretend about any more.

I'm fine, I said. We're both fine.

She nodded. Jason came to see us, she said.

I know, I said.

He would have loved to see you, you know, she said. Your dad. He kept asking me if I thought you'd come and see him.

I said I didn't know. I told him we'd done what we could. I said if she wants to see us she'll come and see us, it's up to her now, there's nothing else we can do.

Don't react, I told myself, don't say anything. But I was also wondering, maybe you're overdoing it? She's an old woman, she's lost her husband. Yes, she was a terrible mother. Or was she really that bad? Maybe it was your fault. But then she threw me out. Yes, but maybe – And this was familiar, it always went like this, me reasoning things through, questioning myself.

It's like when your Granddad was in the hospital, she said. Before he went, and he asked to see all of you – Stephen and Eric and Jim and Paul and you.

I nodded. I remembered rushing home from school that afternoon, his weak papery hand, and the bright lights in the ward.

Though really I expect he meant Jim and Paul, she said.

What? I said.

You know, she said, because Paul's the eldest and he and Jim were close.

I was still confused. Why wouldn't he mean me? I asked. He said me, didn't he?

Yes, Mum said. She wrapped her hand around her mug again, and let it go. I know, she said. Her voice was calm, completely reasonable. I just mean that he probably meant Paul and Jim, that's all.

Why would you even say that? I said. What does it

mean? Why would he say me if he didn't mean me? He loved me.

She shook her head, and her face became disapproving. You're getting at me, she said. You're getting upset. I don't understand. You said you wanted to come and talk. I made your favourite cake. We were having a nice time. I thought we were past all this now. At a time like this.

She was quiet, a little old lady, white-haired, small, at her kitchen table.

You know you'll never win, don't you? said the voice in my head. Stop trying.

But, I thought, but, but. She can't have meant it. Even she –

But you know I loved Granddad, right? I said. There were tears in my eyes. And I used to go over and spend time with them on my own, before I was old enough to go to town alone? When Jim –

All I'm saying is he was specially fond of Jim, and Paul, she said. That's all I'm saying.

But why would he have said me if he didn't mean me?

Oh Claire. She got up and began clearing away her mug, little tottering chunky old shape moving towards the sink. You always have to make so much out of everything, she said.

I've got to go, I said. Relief was washing all over me. So you didn't make it up. You see? Jason, I said.

He's a nice boy, she said.

Of course he is, I thought. He's a boy, isn't he?

He came to see us, before your dad –

A tear rolled down her face. I watched myself watching her cry. She dried her hands on the tea towel, standing near the door while I put on my jacket.

Well, bye, Mum, I said.

Thanks for stopping by, she said, making everything clear.

I made my mouth smile and bent to kiss her cheek. You weren't wrong, said the voice, you weren't wrong, you're not mad, it happened, it's true.

Jason wasn't home when I got back. I made steak and kidney pie, his favourite.

Do you think she's all right? he asked me when we were eating. On her own?

She's not on her own, I said. She's got them. She's always all right, I said. I thought of her, the set of her mouth, her catalogues of things people had done that she didn't like, going back to the Dark Ages. She's never all right, I said. And it's always someone else's fault.

Jason got up and put his plate in the sink. It's not her fault, he said. It's just the way she is. His face was blank and young.

That's true, I said, but it was after he'd left the room. It's just the way she is. I didn't know why it was so heavy, why I had to take it so seriously.

24

Summer doesn't have a date

Jason's not here, I said.

Oh, right, he said. He didn't move.

Do you want to come in and wait? I said. I wouldn't ask everyone, but Jason and Steve are always in and out of here and Steve's house. Cup of tea? I said. I've been in the garden.

Thanks Claire, he said. He followed me through to the kitchen. The floor felt cool and smooth. I was wearing a vest and shorts, and I didn't have shoes on. It had just got too hot to be indoors and be comfortable. The carpets were like radiators. It couldn't last.

What do you want to drink? I asked. Tea? There might be some juice. Or squash.

Tea sounds good, he said. He hung around while the kettle boiled. We took the mugs outside. Do you want a chair? I asked. I just sit here. I sat back on the grass which looked sad and too long, my legs hanging on to the patio.

Here's fine, Steve said. As usual, he was easy to have around. Not just because he was a kid, or I'd known him forever. When did we produce these handsome young men? I thought. Sandra, Steve's mum, and I were new mums together, we met at playgroup. She's a strange one.

How's your mum?

She's all right. She's the same.

I nodded. This garden needs things doing to it, I said. I should mow the lawn at least.

Jason'll do it for you. Steve smiled.

Oh really, I said. I finished rolling and lit up. You look after things for your mum, do you?

Course, he said. He smiled, though.

We sat there with a bumble bee buzzing round and a radio next door, someone's paddling pool and splashing sounds.

So how's things? I asked. What are you planning?

Dunno. College probably. While I think about what to do. I feel like getting a job.

But what about five years from now, ten years, when you don't want to do the same job any more?

I know, he said. How are you supposed to know what's going to happen?

I laughed. Fair enough, I said. I wanted to add, It's less exciting than you think. But I didn't. I tried to remember if I'd been as young as him, when I was that age. They're all so confident now. They know their way around. What's it like, still to be in the part of your life where you think you'll be making decisions about the future?

I'm sorry about your dad, he said.

I thought of the waxy face in the coffin. He'd looked smaller. Maybe he'd got smaller, before. Thanks, I said. You know we didn't really see them, I didn't really see them, for ages.

Do you think that'll change now? he asked.

I shrugged. I dunno, I said. I went to see my mum but – I dunno. We'll see.

Sorry, Steve said again.

It's fine, I said. I felt like lying down on the rug and I did. He lay a foot away from me. I looked at the sky, bleached but still blue. There was a long white line in it, a jet trail. Summer … I thought, and remembered the school field and Katie. Summer doesn't have a year or a date, it just appears and disappears, and while it's happening it's endless. I felt tired, almost drunk. Light-headed.

A hand went over mine on the rug. It was warm, not sweaty, larger than I'd have expected, if I'd thought about it. Everything's going to be all right, Steve said.

I know, I said. I closed my eyes.

25

From the doorway

The thing was that I never felt funny in front of him. I didn't hold in my stomach. I didn't worry about what he'd like or not like. When he tried to fit in four different positions during one shag – doggy style, then holding up one of my legs and tilting me off the bed while he stood up, then being on top of me from behind, then making me sit on him – I finally just told him to stop. I didn't want to embarrass him, but I said, Steve, what have you been watching?

He went bright red.

Jesus Christ, I said. What do all of you watch? What do you think sex is? I imagined Jason doing this to some girl. Maybe she'd like it. More likely she'd be wondering, like me, what the hell was going on.

I'm not trying to be horrible, I said. It just isn't doing anything. It feels weird.

He looked exhausted, like he was going to cry. Mistrust moved across his face.

It feels like you're just doing something and it isn't about me at all, I said. I wasn't angry. I was trying to explain because it mattered that he knew. He sighed and lay down next to me, then rolled over and put his head on my breast. I was about to carry on talking when I realised he was asleep.

Maybe this is what it was like for Damian. I didn't miss Steve. I was happy when I got to see him. I didn't think about him when he wasn't there, except for worrying about Jason, but Jason was after some girl, and he was hardly home. I told Steve he could never tell anyone.

I'm legal, he said.

Yeah … That's not the point, I said. Just don't. We'll both be sorry if you do. Think about your mum, I said, and he held up a hand.

All right, all right, he said.

The fifth time, which was the last time, I ran into him when I was just walking. Out past the wood and around, down towards the football ground. He was coming the same way and ran after me. Cup of tea? I said. Sounds good, he said. For some reason, I don't know why, just before we passed a bus stop he took my hand. There were two old ladies there. As we walked past one said, Nice to see a young man who's not embarrassed by his mother. The other one said something else quietly. I twitched my hand. What are you doing? I hissed.

Nuthin, Steve said. He swaggered a bit.

I yanked my hand away. Don't be stupid, I said.

You don't get to talk to me like that, he said. He stood near the gate of our house, smoking and sulking.

Come inside, I said. I unlocked the door, and went in, leaving it open. Course he followed me to the kitchen. I opened the back door. It was a grey day, bits of sun aching out, but it was warm. I looked down. One of my sandals had been rubbing on my little toe. I filled the kettle.

I made the tea quite slowly. We sat at the table, on each side of a corner. From the open door I heard insects, and a lawnmower. I took off my watch, nearly reached for the paper, and stopped myself. Look, I began to say in my head. You knew this couldn't last.

Steve said, Can we do it one last time then?

I thought about us, tangled in the bobbly cotton-blend sheets, and the box of tissues near the bed, and wrapping the used condom in six plastic bags before throwing it away, and afternoon sun on the wall from a tiny bit where the curtain didn't cover the window. I saw it from the doorway, as though I was looking in. It interested me that I saw myself, not perfect looking, not perfectly thin or big-breasted or anything, messed up, sweaty, and thought I looked sexy. I suppose a person having sex just is sexy, isn't she?

It was the last time, so I stopped worrying about Steve and what he'd think or how he'd feel. I just told him what to do, how to touch me, and he did. It was good. Afterwards we lay there quietly. Then he turned around and said, That was the best one. We looked at each other and I laughed, and he smiled too, and got up and put on his shorts. When he was doing up his belt I heard the door.

Shit! I said.

It's okay, he said. He grabbed his shirt and went out of the room before I could say anything. I thought I was having a heart attack, I breathed so little, or maybe so much. I moved faster than I remember ever moving. The carpet was rough under my feet and I was in my clothes and brushing my hair and on the bed with a magazine maybe a minute later when I heard Jason's voice at the same time as the flush.

Mum?

Yeah?

He came in and I took off my glasses.

Is someone here?

Steve came to see you, I said. I think he's in the kitchen.

He looked at me. The bathroom door opened.

Jason stuck his head out of the door of my room. All right, mate? he said.

I heard Steve saying something about going round to someone's nearby and being on his way and the evening and Jason laughing and then Jason came back in and said quickly, Going out, Mum, see you later.

I thought about shouting after him, What about tea?

Don't overdo it, I thought. I lay down and let my heart stop racing.

26

Higher faster

Jason had his birthday party. I'd talked about it at work and when we were out smoking, John said, You don't want to be home for that. You want to let him and his friends have the house to themselves.

And wreck it? I said.

He smiled and looked down at his shoe, scrubbed the toe on a bit of grass in a crack in the tarmac. Nah, he said, they won't wreck it. We should go out for a drink that evening. Give you something to do. Isn't there a friend you could stay with?

Maybe Katie, I said.

He smiled. That's it. That'd be nice, wouldn't it?

I laughed. I looked at his open friendly face and remembered what I like about men. It's easy for them to be themselves. They throw on a t-shirt, they laugh things off.

At the end of it all I'm too much of a girl. I get caught up in stuff. Maybe, I said.

First John and I went for a couple of drinks in the Hat and Feathers, that quiet old pub down the hill. And this was the best part of the evening. We played pool. I hadn't played in ages. When I play with someone I'm trying to impress I play terribly. I wasn't trying to impress John and I played all right. For an hour or two we had the bit with the table to ourselves and in between shots we chatted, just relaxed. John was telling me about where he lives, his house, and the things he wanted to do to it – do up the attic maybe, paint the walls, get rid of the stuff he'd moved in with. I knew he'd been with someone for a while but I couldn't remember when that was.

Did you move in there with your partner? I said.

No, he said. After we split up – three years ago. He smiled. New start.

Cool, I said.

I guess John and I had never really had a long conversation before, just the two of us, but the fact that I see him every day, and we sometimes have little chats in between smoking, made it seem like nothing. But suddenly he was there, really there. I thought, oh, I like this person. Maybe we could be friends.

When Katie got there I was sure he'd notice her. Men always do. She's good at being noticed, she takes up the space around her. She arrived and hugged me, smiled at John, said finally she was getting to meet someone else who worked at the mysterious fairy-tale shoe factory. That made him grin. Right, she said, what are we drinking? Pool, is it? Great. She got more drinks, rolled up her sleeves, and we started playing, me and her against John. She cleaned up. Near the end there was a shot I had to take – a long one. I'd got distracted listening to the two of them, and wondering what Katie thought of John, or John of Katie. The red ball, our ball, was near a yellow one.

I'm not going to make this, I said.

Think positive, Katie said.

You'll get it, John said. Nice and easy. I looked over at him in the corner, in his old cartoon t-shirt, easy-going. Okay, I said to myself. I hit the ball cleanly, but it stopped just at the lip of the pocket.

Nearly! Katie said.

Unlucky, John said.

I laughed, and said it didn't matter.

Are you starving? I'm starving, Katie said.

I am, I said. Should we head off?

We said bye to John on the way. He smiled at us. Nice to meet you, Katie, he said. See you tomorrow Claire, fingers crossed for the party.

I think it'll be all right, I said.

Katie put her arm through mine as we walked. What do you want for tea? she said.

I don't know, what do you want to do?

Takeaway? He seems lovely.

He's nice, yeah, I'd never really got to know him before, I said, outside work.

She raised her eyebrows.

Oh, come on, I said.

He's nice, she said. I like him. What about that other guy then?

The next afternoon when I was going home I thought about Damian again, and about my dad. Dad going had wiped Damian out of the picture. Almost. Last night at Katie's, after talking about it, I'd dreamt of them both, Dad and Damian, together. Damian put a book in my hand and said, Look after this a minute. I saw him go into a pub. I was just standing there, under the flyover. Later he passed on his way and I tried to give him the book but he didn't want to talk about it. It was a big book, with a red cover. I don't know what it was. Then I saw my dad go by, sad and small, shrunken, his head down. I called after him, but he looked at me as though he was afraid.

The house was tidy enough, the carpets had been vacuumed. There was only a vague smell of smoke. Jason was out. The glass recycling bin was full, and smelled sour. A sunny day. College started next week, and he'd agreed to try it for a year. I made some tea, realised I didn't want it, and sat on the sofa. The smell of the air, and the last warmth of the year, was on my mind. I wanted to move. I thought about the wood. I found myself putting on plimsolls and leggings and a t-shirt. I tied up my hair and left, excited or nervous like someone'd see me. Like I was going to meet someone or something. First I jogged slowly. By the end of the road I'd got into it, and didn't care much when I passed a woman then a couple of kids outside the shop. Near the hill I started really running, like when I was a kid, racing just because I could. I flew up to the park and across it, down to the gate of the wood and along the path, through bushes and the backs of garages. A kid smoking and texting looked up at me but I looked away and he did too. I wanted to laugh I felt so good. Back into the wood and down a slope through the main path out the other side and near the cemetery. I felt a bit sick when I stopped. My face was hot and my lungs were going but it was good. I ran up the little lane and stopped just inside the cemetery.

You could hear birds singing. It sounded like water from a tap. I walked through the first part of the cemetery. It's not so nice, all black and grey stones, 1991 2003 Derek Smyth beloved husband of etc. Dad's funeral. There's something terrible, something false about new headstones. The grass was damp and those steel flower holders on the graves looked dirty and wet. I got my breath back and walked through that leafy tunnel and the other bits of the older graveyard. The private tombs, some falling down. The older stone looked prettier, spotted like the backs of Gran's hands. I went all the way to the little chapel with the pointy roof and the trees round it, then I came back.

On the way home through the park and down the hill I

felt different, older, stranger. I tried to think about how I was running, lift my feet, but my legs were tired especially above the ankles. One hip started hurting for fuck's sake and even my arms no idea why it's not like I'd been running on my hands though the idea made me smile and I put on a spurt down the hill lifted my knees higher faster like we used to in track and got all the way to the main road and our street. Someone in a blue hoodie and jeans turned near the door. Mum? he said. I only stopped when I was on the garden path.

What the fuck are you doing?

Exercising, I said.

You what? But he grinned. I'm so hungover, he said.

Just open the door, I said. I'd lost my flight. I felt heavy. I was thinking about the wood again when I went to the kitchen to get some water. I had to put on the light, it was getting late. The wood felt like a place you could get beaten up or raped even. Something about it. Maybe all old woods are like that. People walk through on their way out all the time, girls too. I've seen them dressed up, small skirt high heels taking the short cut even at night. I wouldn't do it. The wood's different after dark, magic. All the soft hidden places become strange.

27

Like sugar

John and I started seeing each other, which didn't mean shagging. Just seeing each other. It's a funny thing to say, isn't it? We'd been seeing each other every day for years. Then we started spending time together after that night, Jason's party. At first I didn't think about it. He was just someone I'd known forever and we liked each other's company. His family's from Sheringham way. He spoke with that little lift in his voice. He made a certain face when he smiled. He raised an eyebrow. He was easy-going, a person who wouldn't snap, or disappear. I didn't feel mad excitement about him. I just knew he was there. I knew all his clothes: the Hot Tuna t-shirt, the Diesel jeans, the Carhartt jeans, the old suede Converse trainers, the Vans. Clothes the skaters used to wear in school. They still seemed nice, but funny as well. He'd manage things in his own quiet way. He'd buy the first drink. If we went to the cinema he'd be waiting with the tickets. He'd shrug and say he got there early. He'd be on time. I'd be late. He'd be relaxed. Sometimes I'd catch him looking. Then he'd just smile.

I started taking it for granted. I didn't want to. I didn't want to think about anyone that way, feel that if they weren't there I wouldn't be happy. I'd started, not to be happy, but not to think about being unhappy.

Are you going out with John? Jason asked. Friday, September: one of those long, golden days that are even more beautiful than summer. The evening had turned to rain, and the windows gone smeary. I saw a couple of people hurrying past. Jason was going out with Chloe, his new girlfriend. She seems nice, the two times I've seen her. He hasn't brought her round or anything, not to meet me, I mean. She looks sweet, under the make-up.

We're meeting up, yeah, I told him. Going out with sounded a bit specific.

My son grinned.

What, I said.

He's sweet on you, he said.

Since when do you say things like sweet on you, Jason? I asked. You sound like my granddad.

He grinned again. Sweet like sugar, he sang. I tried to clip him round the ear, but he dodged it.

28

Bad for you

Coming for a smoke? It was John, smiling at me, just after the bell for morning break.

Er – nah, I said. You go on.

I saw his smile fade. Something was starting to bother me. For example, his Boxfresh t-shirt. It must have been cool twenty years ago. Why are you still wearing that t-shirt? I wanted to say. Why are you so easy-going? I sulked near the closing section pretending to read the paper till break was over. John smiled at me from the coffee machine at lunch-time, but I stared into my book, which I wasn't reading.

When I was walking back to my table at the end of lunch I could feel John looking. I stared ahead and kept going. Tom came over later, during afternoon break. All right, lass? he said. Cutting down?

Eh?

Not smoking so much?

I swallowed. I heard it's bad for you, I said.

He smiled. Who knew?

I know, I said.

When we were walking out, John smiled at me, and said, See you tomorrow. It was like he was showing me that he understood I was in a bad mood, and he wasn't angry, but would leave me alone. Or perhaps he didn't get anything. I smoked on the way home and felt edgy. My throat was dry. I'm tanning myself, I thought. On the inside. Ugh. I thought about John, and the t-shirt, and the fact that his neck was probably too hairy, and his hair was thinning. Who asked him to like me? I couldn't be responsible for him.

This is what you're like, I thought. You can fall for someone if they pay you some attention then act shifty. You just can't deal with it if they stick around.

The wind was cold on my face as I climbed the hill. But, but, I argued, it's the wrong people that stick around, that's the trouble.

I'd never had the chance to get sick of Damian. I still thought about him, imagined him in his car, with a stack of clean shirts in the boot, and his boxes of books, and the other things he kept neat, in order, so he could live his life in that way he has. He just stops off with whoever he's seeing, he gets love like a cat gets food, here and there. The world provides.

Why couldn't I be like that? Driving around, able to live on whatever comes up. I turned on to our road, and the fat grey cat from the end of the street beetled past, a dark shape on short legs. I saw the gate of our house. Even cats have homes, I thought: at least, the happy ones do. Damian must have someone, somewhere, at least one. A wife, some little Damians, boys or girls. Someone who washes and irons his shirts, reminds him to get enough sleep, smoke less. Someone to spend bank holidays with.

I got to the gate. The front garden looked fucked. I needed to do something to it, or nag Jason to. I picked up a couple of the crisp packets people always throw in when they're passing. It was easier for me to spend time in my mind with Damian, I thought, as I got to the door and opened it – to tell him things, the kinds of things I thought about all day, the little things that happened, that I'd never actually told him and which he'd given no sign of wanting to listen to – than to think about John, admit the possibility of John. But John was easy to have around as things were. I didn't have to improve myself for him, even if he did wear that old t-shirt and have a hairy neck. I didn't care what he thought of me, or I didn't worry. We had a laugh. From the door, taking off my jacket, I caught sight of the sofa in the living room, with a magazine and a couple of DVDs on it, Jason's shoes on the floor, flung anyhow. For a moment I thought I saw a man there, the man to whom the shoes belonged. It was just a second, a trick of the eye. I shut the front door.

29

Closing time

Sometimes the shoes I check don't fit as well with each other as they would with another left, another right. The same model, but something doesn't match. I rearrange them and find another one where the rosette's slightly off-centre, or the shape of the vamp mirrors the other one. It's a small thing. Who'd notice? But it's satisfying, finding the right partner.

After work on Friday I went home and got ready, then I met John at the cinema. We hadn't been out for a couple of weeks, and I'd started to miss him. He hadn't been unfriendly. He still smiled and said hi. He just didn't suggest doing anything after work, didn't come to talk to me. In the end I found myself walking up to him and asking what he was doing that evening. It felt natural. We were friends. Obviously.

After the film we went for a drink, and another drink. He was wearing a jumper I liked, dark grey. I think he might have shaved again. He looked smooth, and in the day I thought I'd seen little points of beard on his cheeks. They're white or blond and they catch the light like sand.

I noticed something. At first when we met he was talking, all natural, but he was holding his arms against his chest, tight. They say that's a sign of wanting to protect yourself, don't they? I found myself doing it back. Two nervous people in a noisy pub, hugging themselves. After a few minutes I told myself to stop doing it, and he did too. I almost felt sorry for him. Then we just talked – about work, about Helen and her husband, and how he always comes to meet her. I said it was sweet, but who'd be like that now? John just smiled.

He told me about the painting he did, and how he'd set up a shed in his garden for it and for playing the guitar, or making music on the computer. I can do what I like out there, he said. It's my own private space. It wouldn't disturb anyone. And he looked at me as though I'd be the person being disturbed.

Who's there to be disturbed? I said. I didn't mean it rudely, but it didn't come out nice. Suddenly I noticed all around us the signs and offers – coffee and a croissant on a weekday morning, Sunday brunch, happy hour, and everyone's clothes, the little logos on them, their trainers, the sides of their spectacles. I felt myself blur into the general Saturday nightness of it all. That way when you're in a pub on a busy night you feel like part of something bigger, which has its own brain, or no brain, a general pissedness, a batteredness the shouting the laughter the mood a swell of it a soap bubble everyone's inside. Someone's elbow her big shiny bracelet someone else's shirt his watch his bald head John opposite me my pint his pint the table the beermat someone's shoes the pub carpet and closing time.

Before I thought about it John and I were walking up the road to my house. I didn't ask him to come home with me, but I didn't tell him not to. What are you going to do about this, now, I asked myself, but most of all I'd had enough to drink, more than, and I was tired and I wanted to go home. The rest would sort itself out. I didn't want to have to explain anything ever again.

Two hours and two spliffs later, John and I were in my bed. We hadn't done anything – every time he inched towards me on the sofa, I'd inched away, but without saying anything. He hadn't asked. It was a miracle. I rolled myself up in my half of the duvet. Goodnight then, I said.

30

About right

Claire?

Not now, I thought. I pulled myself out of the edges of sleep. Yeah, I said. I heard myself sounding like the mother of a three-year-old.

Are you asleep?

Half, I said. I turned around, almost on my side. All right? I said.

John, still in his t-shirt and jeans, smiled. Yeah, he said. How are you?

I'm all right, I said. I didn't move towards him. I kind of wanted him to kiss me, or want to. And I didn't want to do anything. Damian, I thought.

We spent a while looking at each other. I hadn't noticed, but there were orange bits in his eyes. Hazel eyes with orange bits. Is that a sign of insanity? Suddenly everything meant something, and all of it was probably something I should take into account.

Can I come a bit closer? John said.

I sighed. All right, I said. The truth was, I did sort of want a hug. I didn't want to do anything I couldn't take back later. I didn't want him either to go or to get too close. This was about right.

He got closer, moved some hair out of my face, and kissed me quite gently. I kissed his top lip. It tasted fine. I put my bottom lip between his, and he bit it. He put his hand on my breast and squeezed it, felt my back, stroked my stomach. I kind of liked it. I felt I could get turned on, if I stopped stopping myself. Damian's face floated before me. If I let myself get turned on now, would it be because of Damian? Did it matter?

John rolled on top of me. Am I crushing you? he asked.

No, I said. I lay still. Don't ask, I prayed. Don't ask what's going on. I stroked his arm, and felt the muscles in it. He sighed. He rolled to the side and tried putting his hand down my pants. I seemed to be in my underwear, and pyjamas. It was morning. At some point Jason would come back from Chloe's, maybe with Chloe. On the other hand it was a nice day, so maybe they'd go out. Anyway, that wasn't the point ... I twisted to the side and John moved his hand. We stopped looking at each other.

After a while he said, Are you hungry?

I dunno, I said. How about a cup of tea? A bit later I

got up and made tea. Then I made breakfast, and we sat and talked about work, and laughed about people there, for a long time, till late in the afternoon. After he'd left, with a hug, I thought about John. It seemed easier to let myself feel close to him when he'd gone.

I tried to remember how it had been with Pete, and it seemed so far away. We were so young. I thought things would always be that simple. You liked someone and they liked you and it just happened. But it hadn't been like that later. Was it even possible for anything to be new any more? I thought about it that evening when I went to bed early. I'd changed the sheets and they were soft. I stretched out and felt good about the fact that someone had been there, nearby, so I didn't have to feel alone, but wasn't there now, so I could be at peace. Every experience reminded me of something else, in a good way, this is better than before, or a less good way, this isn't as good. Like a form I had to fill in stating defects. Faults other people might not notice. Even the perfect product, the perfect shoe, whatever that meant, it might not be something you fancied. You just wouldn't be able to argue it wasn't right. It depended on what you were looking for, and that depended on what you were used to, so the same things kept repeating. I fell asleep and dreamed of shoes, and signs in pubs, and parts of people: shirts, the backs of heads, bags, skirts, but all separate, all floating. I woke in the evening for a bit and heard voices. Jason and Chloe. My throat hurt. I was in the middle of making a noise. I put my face back in the duvet.

In the morning before I knew it was morning or that I was me or where I was or who was being there, it was the light I felt. It must have come through the curtains and on to my face and through my eyelids. I didn't know any of that. I was just aware of the light, forcing its way through, and once it was there, that there had been darkness, which had to give way.

IV

Chappals

6

In the dark

With half an ear I listened to the radio. She was out; dusk was falling. I sat on the edge of the bed, feeling tired.

This is the Voice of Heaven, and you're listening to …

In the eighties Chinese transistor radios appeared everywhere. A few years later, the television. At first they were rented for special occasions, then people started having them at home. Deepak offered to get us one, but I didn't want it. Later, when they got a new one they gave us the old one. She likes to watch in the evening. But when I'm alone I turn to the radio. That voice has always been with me, promising a message that will change everything, make me understand.

Why are you sitting in the dark?

She switched on the light as she said it, put something down, went to the kitchen. I used my fists to push myself up and followed. She was reheating a bhaji, the rice, the daal. Were you hungry? she said. You could have eaten.

Where did you go?

I went to see Prakash.

Oh. I moved some things on the counter, hung up the pakad at which she turned and said, I need that. Pass me the fodni spoon.

I reached for it and my back twinged. Aah.

She took the spoon from me and poured in the oil. I watched the flame lick the sides of the spoon, the oil begin to smoke.

You haven't asked how he is, she said.

What?

Hiss! The jeera flew into the oil and began to smoke.

Your son, you haven't asked how he is.

I stared at her. She seems smaller. She's still slender, but the skin around her arms has slackened. Now, her air of energy has a wintery quality.

Do you happen to have any idea what he was up to? I asked. I put the jeera back where it belongs.

The garlic went into the oil. It began to crackle and fry.

Too hot, I said.

She ignored me.

The oil, I said. Perhaps she was tired. I certainly was. Well, I said, how is he?

His face is very swollen, she said sadly. Near the eye. And his mouth.

What was he thinking? I said. He's so hot-headed. All of this came about simply because of drinking.

What would you know? she said. I could tell from her voice that she was infuriated. It's rare that she engages with a feeling instead of stepping around it.

It's obvious, I said. It's motivated by thuggishness. You don't know about men. There are different ways of going about things. Look at Deepak. He would never do something like this.

With a hiss the fodni went into the daal.

We ate in silence. I wasn't feeling good, and I went straight to bed. She watched television for a while, I think, not long. The next time I woke the room was dark. I was thirsty and weary, and there was a dull ache in the pit of my stomach, or lower. For a moment I felt warm, and the old terror returned, the fear of having soaked the bed. My brother jumping up, kicking me, muttering something. My mother complaining. It happened only a few times, but it became part of my reputation. At your age, said my mother, as though I'd decided to indulge in an unsavoury habit. It was discussed in front of people: Arun still wets the bed. I'd stare at my feet. Once, I remember, it was my father who woke when I stumbled up. Here, he said calmly. Give me the sheet. You two go to the tap. He was soon behind us, rinsing out the sheet and the thin mat on which we slept. A short while later we were asleep again.

When I woke, late, the dull pain was still there. I missed

my father, and my mother. I wanted to go home, to a home I wasn't sure had ever existed.

I lay still for a few minutes, feeling heavy, as though after a blow.

Then I got up, everything creaking, and went out. I was desperate, but only a brief, burning trickle emerged. I began to go back inside, then once again was sure I hadn't finished, so returned to the outhouse and leaked a few hot drops.

I don't feel well, I told her as I came in.

I'll heat your tea.

I don't feel well, I said. I went to lie down.

In the time that followed nothing had edges. Feelings massed: the pain in my lower back, tiredness, thirst, the need to urinate, the fear of that burning.

I heard her ask if she should call someone. Who would she call?

I thought of my father. In dreams he was always walking somewhere, restless. In the last few dreams he had been carrying a single chappal. The dead are not at rest or is it we who –

The smell of parijatak. There is a bush in the garden. Sometimes my mother wears a flower in her hair. The scent is so sweet and sad, my favourite of the puja flowers.

In the morning she likes to go to the field temple. It's a

familiar walk, only half an hour. It's the walk I like, though the place is pleasant too, the little shrine and the three enigmatic black stones, Narsoba and his wives. I forget the story but they must have been found nearby. Cucumber vines in the field we walk through to reach the temple, their tangle and ripeness, and the green smell. In the monsoon a woman is leaning over a tank and washing them before they are taken to market. We smile at her; she smiles back.

I don't feel well. I don't feel well. My back aches. And an image of the compounder's shop where my father would go if we were sick, to get medicine. Its counter was lit against the evening. Feeling ill and waiting for him to return, tense with the cost of the medicine, which my mother would point out as I stood, shaky, clutching his hand.

Some distance after the temple, but in the same area, there is an abandoned well. My friend Suresh and I find it. The well is deep, with steps inside, and the water is far below, dank. One summer we go there every afternoon.

Eh re, look at this, Suresh says. What is it? Is it a pit?

I think it's a well.

But it's so quiet and dark. He is leaning over the edge.

It smells bad, I say.

Let's explore it –

In the middle of this I saw my wife, a silent, severe figure sitting next to me. No, that's not right. Not severe. Just waiting for me to be better.

It won't happen, I told her.

What won't?

She sat there and I missed my mother. I wished my wife would hold my hand.

I'll never be the person you want me to be, I said.

Don't think of me, she said. Think of your son.

I waved my hand. He –

You should think of him, he needs you.

He's a grown man, I tried to say.

Should we go to the doctor?

No. There's something I have to tell you, I said.

What?

Wait. I pushed myself up and wobbled out to the latrine. Everything was too bright. I saw the neighbour's son, playing with an old bicycle wheel and a stick. He stared at me. His grandfather, a decrepit white-haired man who sits on a disused handcart, reading the newspaper, perhaps feeling that it is his private place, even the old man lifted his head and stared.

Yes, I thought, take a good look. Finally something is happening.

I was back in bed. She was nearby. Shall I call someone, she said.

Who would you call? I said. Everyone relevant is dead. Soon I'll be dead too. Listen, there are some things I have to say. That whole business with Ratna, you didn't know about it, but I don't want you to misunderstand. Things happen. There's your real life, and then there are other things – like being delayed on a journey or something. They don't count. I mean –

The well is by a ruined house through the middle of which grows a peepal tree. The house used to belong to an Englishman in olden times. Now the walls are broken, and before it there are open fields. Behind, the jungle has started coming back.

Suresh says, The well probably has diseases. Ghosts.

Jump in and find out, I say.

You jump in.

Maybe there's a snake at the bottom, I say, a huge snake.

A python?

A water python.

Throw this in.

A stick flies through the air. A long time later, a faraway sound.

I'm going to climb in, I say. Immediately I regret it. I turn, because it's important to show no fear, climb the lip, and begin to descend the dark steps.

The smell. Fertile, green. The stone under my feet is slimy and somehow sad. The steps curve down.

It is the first time in my short life I have been alone. The light at the top becomes whiter and more distant. The smell and the silence, apart from my footsteps and their echo, preoccupy me. What am I? I've never considered it. I've accepted myself as an adjunct to my brother, an extra set of limbs that at night grow on to his side.

Before I started going down I thought of lies to tell Suresh. There actually is a huge snake at the bottom, with enormous green eyes. There are fish, like in a pond, but much bigger, their mouths splitting the skin of the water. But as I continue to climb down, these ideas leave me. All that remains is the stone, my feet and hands, the steps, and the wall of the well: the light as it disappears in whiteness and reappears below in gleams of blue and grey in the black.

It feels as though I am descending to an emotion as much as a location: as though sadness has collected in the bottom of the well. The water smells bad, not green and dark but just of death. I have the urge to allow myself to fall. Hearing nothing above, I stay still and wait to find out what to do. I think of the monsters I was going to tell Suresh about, and the water's dark invitation.

I crouch against the wall. My legs hurt, especially my knees. I straighten, slowly, and begin to shake as the blood returns to my feet.

But I've started climbing too fast. Halfway, I put my foot where the next step should be, and slip, a slip I have been anticipating. I cry out and cling to the wall. Blood pounds through my ears. I want to scream for my mother.

In a minute or two my breathing becomes normal. I put out my hand to feel for the next step, and carry on climbing. But the moment of fear remains, a terrible event I have had to go through.

Near the top I hear Suresh's excited voice. He helps to

pull me out, and starts to ask questions, but I put out my hand.

Are you sick? Do you feel unwell?

I look at the sky, and the trees with their leaves, think of my parents in our home and how I believed I would never see them again. They wouldn't find out what happened to me until it was too late. Now I am safe but I know that it is possible for me to experience things they will never know about, and that I will have to keep doing this. I close my eyes.

7

The living

You're awake? A tall dark man was looking at me. His shoulders were broad, his face shifty, but there was something nearly noble about him. He stood.

He's awake! he called towards the kitchen.

What are you doing here? I mumbled. No work?

Sunday.

Oh. But – I started to say.

Anil came in. Your food will be ready soon, he said, important with the message. He smiled. He looks like his mother, this boy. Round-faced. Probably a good thing. I was still trying to think whom my elder son had reminded me of. Someone in my father's family. Perhaps one of the elder brothers, whom we rarely saw, except at big occasions, a wedding in the village. Or a cousin of my father.

My wife came in. How do you feel? she asked, businesslike.

Strange that in this room, she and my grandson were the only people from whom I would have hoped for mercy. Whatever that means.

I don't know, I managed. Why is everyone here? My daughter-in-law had also come in, carrying shopping in her hand.

You were ill. We had to take you to the hospital. You had a fever. Urinary infection. They had to check it hadn't spread to your kidneys.

Oh. But I – Oh, I said. I did remember a ward, very noisy, the smell of disinfectant. I'd thought it was a dream.

Dehydration, said my daughter-in-law loudly from the kitchen.

My grandson had an urgent question. Can I watch TV?

All right, I said. Is there a match? He ran to turn it on.

I don't remember all this, I said to my son. He remained looking at me. He had on a clean kurta, and in effect looked quite handsome, if unlike either of us. Who are these people, who appear in your life and stay in your house, with whom you are forever linked, apparently? How does it happen? It was beyond me. His kindness made me want to weep.

My daughter-in-law came with a plate. I sat up. It was food for invalids: watery doodhi with chana daal; a thin amti, rice, cucumber. Are we all eating this? I wanted to ask. But I began, and it was good. I was soon done, however.

Now your medicine, my wife said. How she appeared in this way, at crucial moments, at the bedside. I swallowed two pills, and lay down again. The batsmen led the players off the field. The cricket commentator was talking in English. Any minute now three or four of them would appear, sitting at a table, in their blazers, with their balding heads, serious men discussing serious things. Anil sat on the floor, rapt, cross-legged, his palms on the ground, gazing up. The television threw a greenish light towards him.

The sound was soft and copious, the air fresh.

It shouldn't be raining now, I said. I sat up a little. I was on the bed, against the wall. The softness of the rain entered the room. I pulled the covers around me. After Ganpati, I said.

It's probably a final shower, she said. She was on the floor, sorting through our bartans. Some of the older ones, copper, needed re-tinning. And she had opened the cupboard to tidy, and taken down from the shelves the various packages wrapped in cloth or secreted in boxes and tins.

What are you doing? I asked. I meant, Is it necessary to dismantle everything? Can't you see I'm vulnerable?

Monday, the first day of the week. Out of habit I looked near the door, but there was no pile of hides. There were no finished chappals tied up with cord. Both had been collected last week.

She said, still pulling things out of the cupboard, This is a good chance to do all this. Ordinarily I don't get time.

Ordinarily meaning, when work is going on, when life is normal. I leaned against the wall. This was the room where I had eaten and slept, so that I could wake up and work. Here I had had sex with my wife, and our children had grown up. None of these things made sense if I wasn't working. I'd felt chained to work, and to my family, to the unending file of things that had to be done – take in the new hides, cut out the soles, wake my sons, help them to bathe, hurry them inside so their mother could feed them, carry on working, listen to the radio, have tea, talk to the man who came to collect the finished work, stick on the soles, sew on the belts, eat lunch, rest for a few minutes, work in the afternoon darkness as the light moved until it was time again for tea, take a walk at sunset with some errand or other to run, go here, collect this, watch the children outside, beat them if they didn't study or if they fought and this not with pleasure but efficiently and rarely.

People dropped in. We went to things – weddings, funerals.

I saw our house, that room, in the evening, in the tube light. The boys at different ages, big then small, eating, talking, working, arguing. Their mother always there. I wasn't in these scenes.

Those moments with Ratna were supposed to flare up and die out. But I found myself thinking about her in between. I was cautious. I didn't want to allow myself too much pleasure. I thought I could try this out for a while, then return to the house, and the old life, my real life, without anyone knowing. No one did know, but the loss I feared crept up on me anyway. It wasn't that my family would find out. It was that I would be different, so that the same things would no longer satisfy me.

When Ratna's husband decided that they should move to his brother's place, somewhere in Karnataka, I wasn't sad. There was no special farewell, no sentiment. I told myself that if it had gone on for longer than a few months, I would have tired of it, of her. And yet I was shaken. Walking home that day, I realised it was a good thing: once again, I had been delivered of my worries before they could become substantial. Then, suddenly, I burst into tears.

Before I got to the door the paan walla told me there had been a call for me at the PCO. I wiped my face and went to find out. It was my brother, the man said. I called back, wondering what was going on. As I listened to his PCO ringing – he must have been waiting near it, as I was, a man on the street – I was aware of the footfalls around me; footfalls, and voices. I was tired. I hadn't slept well the previous night, wondering if I would be able to see Ratna before she left. I hadn't known if we would have the time to have sex. In the event her husband was out, and we did it, quickly, on the floor, in the same place as the first time. The return, a circle closing, struck me, but I looked at her as she lay on my shoulder for a few minutes and said nothing, because we didn't talk about things. As I walked home all the emotion I hadn't allowed myself to feel in the last few months flowed through me. I had been with this woman, and I hadn't known her at all, hadn't let her know me. Sometimes when I'd been apart from her, I'd felt her presence, only a few streets away, in her own house, with her husband, but no children, for she said there was something wrong with her and they weren't able to have any.

Now all that was gone. I was lonely again, amid the sound of footsteps, car horns, lorries, the smell of fumes, the voices of passers-by.

Arun? said Sanjay's voice on the other end of the line.

Yes, I said.

He said it was Atya, our father's elder sister. She'd had a heart attack and been taken to hospital, where she'd had another. It wouldn't be long.

I wasn't expected to do anything, or even say much. He was just telling me. I hung up and went back towards the house.

My aunt was more than ten years older than my father. It had been she, more than his mother, who'd brought him up. She hadn't been in good health since the time we moved. She didn't take care of herself: she liked fried food, late nights, a shot of rum if it was around. She chewed supari and smoked beedis, at times in quantities. No one questioned her, certainly not my uncle. I remember him only vaguely. He was an ordinary man with a gambling addiction. He was pleasant enough: he would give us a few pice, or buy us puffed rice, or a rubber ball.

When I was young, eight or nine, I was a silent, interior person, unperceived by my family. My older brother had a gang of friends and they went out to do teenage things. I was still a child. I remember Atya turning to me during a visit. We were the only two inside. She was cooking and smoking, and stopped to relight her beedi.

You're always watching, Arun, she said. What are you thinking?

Nothing, I said. I don't know.

She shoved a pile of bhindi at me. Here, she said. Make yourself useful. Cut off the tops.

I began to trim the bhindi.

Not like that, she said. Don't take off so much. See? You've wasted this.

I squinted down at the geometric green tubes, and sticky strings of sap.

My aunt turned again to look at me. It was dark, and her back was to the window, so I hardly saw her face. You're too serious, she said. You think too much. You need to be strong to survive in this world. Make the world fit in with you, don't try to fit in with the world. Don't let people make you feel bad.

Before I went into my house that day I thought, there is a certain number of breaths each of us has to take, and no amount of care or carelessness can alter that. I said goodbye, in my heart, to my aunt, and wished her good luck.

As I went in to tell my wife and sons the news I thought that it is the living we should pity, for the life they have yet to go through. There were many nice things in my days. In the morning I enjoyed my tea, and shaving under the tree. When I had been working for a while I liked the moment when I came out of my trance and became aware of the road, the horn of a car, and maybe a bullock cart trundling past; the moment when the world came in through the open door and I realised I would soon be hungry. I liked to sit with a tumbler of water after my lunch and look at the tree behind the house, to feel the sun on my face before I went in again to work. I liked to see my sons laughing, to hear their voices. And yet I thought of Ratna and the fact that she was going for good and knew with certainty that I could die at any time, absolutely without grief. And this thought once again brought tears to my eyes, for reasons I would have found it hard to justify, tears that I passed off as relating to the imminent death of my aunt.

8

Coming and going

She was carrying one or two packages, and other things were piled on the side. There was a cloth near the cupboard.

What are you doing? I said. My voice sounded gravelly.

Everything's gone bad, she said, and went out with an armful of cloth.

What happened, I groaned. I lifted myself on one arm and began to sit up. It was an operation. First I lifted the head. Then I propped myself on one hand. A certain amount of groaning while I straightened. Twinges in the back. And it was done.

She came back, insultingly upright, and squatted next to the cupboard. You've used too much phenyl, I said. The smell's strong.

She looked up. We'll need new clothes for the wedding, she said. These ones have rotted.

Clothes, I said. Who knows if I'll even be well enough. In my mind I saw my niece's face. We must go, I said.

She was looking in the cupboard. Things have been lying here for years, she said. No one looks. No one takes care of anything.

She turned to face me. I did know about you and that woman, she said. How stupid do you think we are? Everyone knew.

I remained frozen on the bed. I wanted to laugh. This is part of the illness, I told myself.

You started talking the other day, remember? Before we took you to the hospital.

I looked down. I don't know what I said, I muttered.

Too much and not enough, she said. As usual.

So you're just going to sneer at me, is that it? I said. You don't understand. You don't want to understand. We should both calm down, I added, remembering that I was ill and this wasn't a good time to pick a fight. I longed for comfort.

She remained staring at me. Suddenly she sat on the floor.

Why are you sitting there? I said. Sit on the bed.

No, she said. After a moment she sighed and put her head on one hand, resting her elbow on her thigh.

Come on, I said. You're making me get up, I added reprovingly. I went to sit opposite her. What is it? I said.

She shook her head. Sometimes I feel so sorry for her. She needs, probably not me, but someone, and there's no one else. Still, I hold myself back, for I'm not getting what I need either. One of us has to grow up, I thought, and immediately began coming up with reasons why it shouldn't have to be me.

After a time she wiped her face, thoroughly, one hand massaging around each eye. She stood.

Come, sit on the bed, I said.

No, she said. I haven't finished my work.

I stood too. Oh, I said, ah. On my way to the outhouse I stopped at the kitchen door. It was years ago, I pointed out. I made a mistake, I added, not completely believing this.

She was herself again. Yes, she agreed. It was years ago.

I walked out and thought, how like her not to say anything. I imagined the life we might have led if I had not been so stupid or selfish, the relationship we might have had, some greater tenderness. I was trembling as I waited in the outhouse, without great result, though I managed to urinate a little. Maybe it's getting better, I thought, shaking myself out. Maybe things will start flowing again. I had been confused, nothing but a child pretending to be a man. I'd thought no one had noticed.

Again I passed the old man in his handcart. He looked up and threw out something hoarse. I waved. But he beckoned me over.

What did you say? I enquired.

How's yourself? he wheezed. I stared. Your health, he said.

I'm all right, I said, it'll be all right. I'm going to be all right. How are you?

I held on to the side of the handcart.

His eyes, sharp and brown but so deeply sunken in the face, looked at me over spectacles. They said you were having trouble with your waterworks, he observed, loudly as though it was I, not he, who couldn't hear. I see you coming and going a lot. He indicated the outhouse. I see you coming and going.

A fleck of spittle landed on my cheek.

I closed my eyes, opened them. The sun was hot on my head. Yes, I said. I have been coming and going more.

He nodded, eyes cunning. It happens, he said. He smiled, a thin smile, to indicate that the conversation had ended, and I went back to my house. Who has any privacy in this world? And yet somehow I'd remained unseen amid it.

I went to lie down, and turned on the radio. The familiar voice began, This is the Voi— but it dwindled and died. I shook the radio, switched it off and on.

The radio's stopped working, I said. She carried on wiping things, lining the cupboard shelves with newsprint.

I realised what I'd been missing. Where's Tuka? I said. I thought he'd come and sleep with me. I haven't seen him all day. Was he there this morning?

She turned then. No, she said.

Where is he? I said. I lay down and felt uneasy. I started to sleep, but a wedding band passed, loudspeakers and cacophony, and a mosquito began to whine near my ear. I missed the radio, and worried about Tuka. He's not young any more.

What if a dog had caught him? Or he'd been run over? My imagination went out to him, wherever he was, injured, hungry, lost somewhere.

9

A tap on the shoulder

As the Sumo pulled away I craned over my shoulder. The house looked small and crumpled, our blue door closed. Most of all I didn't see what I was keenly looking for.

She glanced at me. She knew what I was thinking, but she didn't say the comforting thing: He'll be back, don't worry, or, He's all right, wherever he is.

I sighed. Lately, I don't know when, I have begun to sigh suddenly and deeply. Or maybe I have only noticed it recently. I swallowed down what seemed to be bile and settled myself for the journey.

Next to me, Anil and my daughter-in-law were discussing what would happen at the wedding, and who would be there. My brother's sons and their children; people from the groom's side, and all of us in the house. Deepak and his family would come directly from Pune. I regarded the back of Prakash's head. The Sumo had been his idea. He knew someone; we'd hired it at a discount. It'll be more comfortable, he said, eyeing his decrepit father. I hadn't demurred.

I waited for our first halt, ostensibly for tea, but actually because I wanted to hobble around the back of the dhaba and see what happened. Prakash shot me a glance and stayed in front, chatting to Nitin, the driver. As I came back out I saw Anil, hanging off his father's arm, and singing to himself while spinning around. Prakash carried on talking to Nitin on whose face a pair of sunglasses flashed. He didn't turn, but his hand went down and held his son's shoulder. I saw the satisfaction on the boy's face and felt a pang of envy – at my age – then surprise. How secure his father makes him feel.

Nitin and Anil went to the bathroom and I lowered myself to the wall near which we were parked. Prakash hesitated and sat next to me. We'd left home at eight. Now it was nine thirty. We would arrive in time for lunch. I felt no hurry to get to Miraj. Perhaps I even felt apprehensive. It was so long since I had been there. I gazed at the sunny road, and the sign saying Aashirwad Garden Hotel and Restaurant.

The case has been dropped, Prakash said, and I turned to him.

Oh? I said. I didn't know.

Yes.

Good, I said.

His large hands pushed imaginary sleeves up his forearms. Vigorous arms, the arms of a man in or approaching the prime of his life. When had my prime been? When had the moment happened?

The police, he began. When I was at the police station.

My stomach empty, my bladder for once quiet, I said nothing. The sunlit morning, the heat, the cars passing, and we on our way but not yet arrived, not yet required to fulfil any role, represent anything, it was restful.

When they were – I got beaten up, Prakash said.

Yes, I said.

He gave me a suspicious look, but I'd had nothing else to say.

At the time, he said, it struck me that – I realised something.

Oh? I said. I looked at my right foot. The big nail is misshapen from too many accidents with the hammer.

I realised none of it mattered, he said. Now he too looked at his feet, big and strong, the toes hairy in sports sandals.

I waited.

It really hurt, he said, and there was a note of surprise in his voice. He could have been the boy I remembered, thirteen or fourteen years old.

I patted his shoulder.

There's no – there's nothing like the future, he said.

Was he about to cry? I hoped not. Mm, mm, I said preemptively, wondering what the others could be doing inside for so long. When you travel, routine goes out of the window.

You wouldn't ordinarily allow your child to stuff himself with fried food, but the usual rules stop operating.

Prakash turned to me. His eyes found mine. Nothing matters, he repeated. We don't affect anything. The reasons we think we do things … He looked down. Nothing matters.

Mm, I said.

I've been thinking, I might go on the wari next year.

You?

Yes. Suddenly he looked younger.

Oh. Well, I don't know so much about it, but it takes time, doesn't it? And it's not just the pilgrimage. You have to follow some rules. No meat. No alcohol.

He nodded. Yes, I know, he said. I thought it might be good.

I considered my hands. Why did you get into that fight? I asked.

His head moved suddenly towards me and I recoiled. Don't you – you're really asking? he snapped.

Oh, but – after all this time? What would it change? I said. I felt ancient, like someone from another world.

They came out of the dhaba, she and my daughter-in-law and Anil. The boy was having his face wiped. His eyes were glazed.

It seemed later than it was.

*

I was at the sea, at Chowpatty in Mumbai. The air tasted different here – of salt, and freedom. The sea was green, not clear, and the buildings curved like they do in the films. I ate gola that made my throat sore and walked to the edge of the water. There was sand under my feet; I'd taken off my chappals, and was carrying them. I heard voices speaking several languages. The breeze was warm, and savoury.

At the water's edge a wave licked my foot, its touch warm as a cat's tongue. I yelped and moved back, and a couple walking past laughed. The setting sun, its gold and glamour blown by the breeze, glanced off them.

But my neck snapped, and my eyes showed me a road with trees, much closer to home, but changed, and then, with a filmic slowness, suddenly a black motorcycle snaked across our path. The young rider wasn't looking. He was reversing from under a tree. We would hit him straight on.

Not at the last moment, but after it, Nitin made a big turn of the wheel and we shaved past the bike.

Prakash shouted out of the window.

I – I said.

Yes, said my wife.

I was sure we were going to hit him.

Did you notice, she said, how time slowed down?

I saw the black of the bike, and its dancing movement, a cobra rising. There are times you feel something has reached out to tap you on the shoulder.

We entered the town, old and familiar, its rhythm still gentle despite the new buildings of glass and metal.

The house is and isn't the same. Ten years ago the municipality had a scheme to finance rebuilding houses from before a certain year. My brother saved and borrowed. The house he lives in now is therefore a reimagining of our old house, in the same spot, but made new in concrete. It's more comfortable: it even has a bathroom. Yet it's lost the presence of the old house.

In the afternoon, when I'd rested, I was sitting on the bench at the back, facing the yard. This patch of land used to be the limit of the known world. I saw the corner, in which there were now other pukka houses, but where there had been trees, a ditch, and a gap through which Suresh and I would slip out, on our way to an adventure. The parijatak bush must have gone a long time ago.

My brother sat next to me. He didn't say anything, but I felt his thoughts around me.

Everything's ready? I asked.

He nodded. The shamiana, the food, the priest, her clothes, the gifts.

How is she? I said.

Who?

Sangita.

He looked surprised. She's fine. Why?

I don't know, I said. I thought of the groom, a nondescript young man, and of my niece, her calm intelligence.

We had to use a matchmaker, he said. I was relieved, it's been a while. Better get it done quickly, I thought. By Diwali they'll be settled in their house.

She'll live in the village?

He nodded.

There was no one educated?

He snorted. You think it's easy?

No, I said. I mean, I'm sure it's not.

She has the brains her brother should have had, he said.

If she studied more, I said.

Better to get her married before it becomes a problem.

When we talk now, my brother and I, it's not as though we're strangers, but there's the facade of being men. I still find myself expecting tenderness from him, that he will acknowledge how I feel next to him, which is small, in his shadow. But perhaps he only saw me as an interloper, a nuisance.

Well, now … I said.

Yes. He stood. I'd better see what's happening, he said. I'll get them to give you tea.

It was my niece who came with the cup. She smiled and sat down with me. I need to go in a minute, she said.

You're busy, I said.

She looked as if she wanted to roll her eyes.

So, you're looking forward to married life? I said.

My tone was teasing, the way anyone might talk to her, except that she and I have always been close.

She looked surprised. I continued to smile.

How could I know what it's like to be married? she asked.

You've seen your parents, your aunts and uncles, your brothers.

She hugged her knees and looked across the yard. Seeing other people is not the same, she said.

I stopped, embarrassed, as though we were talking about sex.

There was a sound from inside, perhaps my sister-in-law calling her.

Seeing an animal in a cage isn't the same as living in one, she murmured.

What?

She took the cup from me and went in.

10

Two plastic chairs

I hate weddings. I looked around at the lights, the halwai's stand, the people in shiny clothes milling in groups. My family as usual had betrayed me. Deepak was smiling and talking to one of his cousins' wives. I couldn't see Prakash. Anil was running round with the other children. I was in a corner with a decrepit old man. These days, I attracted them, I suppose because like them I needed a plastic chair to sit on, slightly outside the main scrum.

This one must have come with the groom's party. I didn't know him. He sat gazing rheumily into the middle distance, holding a cup of Fanta. He didn't smell bad, only vaguely of mothballs. The future, I told myself, and felt amused, then appalled, for it was the present.

I crossed my legs, uncrossed them because it's bad for the back, crossed them again, tried to sit straight, gave up and slumped, feeling, as a person in a chair at the edge of a party does, that no one could see me, but everyone else was somehow there for my viewing.

Suddenly I blinked. This figure coming towards me – he was bald, or nearly, and older too. He looked awful. His shoulders were lopsided, his chest weak and slack, his gait rickety, yet purposeful. I knew him at once. How hadn't I thought of seeing him? Where had he been all this time?

In a moment, he was bending down to the old man in white. Arun? he said.

Eh, Suresh! I said. He turned when he heard my voice. I was a foot or two behind, slightly in shadow. Oh, he said, trying to disguise his surprise. There you are!

I got up hastily, pushing the arms of the chair. Here, I said, and grabbed his elbow. Come on.

I piloted Suresh out of the wedding area and towards, I didn't know where, but the back of the yard. He didn't protest.

You thought that was me? I said. You're incredible.

He giggled. I nearly slapped him hard, like in the old days.

Eh? I persisted.

They said you were in the back sitting down, he said. I haven't met you in years. Don't take it too seriously. You always thought too much.

You – I tried to hit him but he laughed and moved away.

It's good to see you, Arun, he said.

It's good to see you too, I said. Though I can't see anything. Where are we going?

There's still an exit here.

We were back in the old place. But our bolthole was now between two pukka houses. Some of the scrub was there. It smelled the same: a little medicinal, a little chemical. I felt as natural as though I'd been slipping down this narrow gully for the last fifty-five years. In dreams perhaps I had.

Where are we going, re? I asked.

Not too far, he said.

We walked along the road, which was dark, he leading with his bandy gait and I following, stumbling, cursing. How far is it? I said. I'll tell you the truth, I haven't been well. I was in hospital for a couple of days, not too long ago.

That's what they told me, he said. But you look all right, much better than –

Than that old man you thought was me?

He laughed his wheezy laugh. I would have looked at another man his age, crumpled, his remaining hair wispy and mad, and his little face wrinkled, and found him absurd, pathetic, and he was, but nothing had changed. Certain loves slip into us before we are able to weigh things up.

But how much further is it, I said. This is really –

Just here, he said. The track divided into three. We took the left side and after a while we came to a small car mechanic's shop. Just a minute, Suresh said.

He disappeared around the back of the shop and re-appeared to call out, Arun! Come.

What's this fellow up to now, I grumbled. But I followed, stumbling on the uneven ground. A machine to check the air pressure of tyres stood in the moonlight, leaning over, a sleeping sentinel.

Suresh had found two plastic chairs and was sitting on one. Here, he said with a grin. He also had a bottle, and near it a rag. I threw back my head and laughed. Trouble was on its way towards me, and it was going to be impossible to resist.

So this is where you keep your stash?

The owner is a friend, Suresh said. Sit down.

I sat on the chair. Well, I said, this is better than the wedding. Although we can't stay long. I must get back before anyone thinks about where I am.

I heard the seal of the bottle being broken, and he passed it my way.

Oh, I said. The moonlight fell across the clear plastic, the yellow label, the fluid inside. I smelled solvent, and oranges. I don't really –

It doesn't matter if you normally do or not, Suresh said. Today is today. We haven't seen each other since whenever, but now we're both here. You have a drink with me.

I looked at him, the earnest eyes, which were unchanged, in the face, which was creasing like brown paper. I nodded.

The air smelled of flowers, and petrol. The back of the mechanic's shop gave on to a ditch, then a field. I miss the country, I said. I don't even think about it. And then when I'm here …

I took a sip of the santra. It was the same, more like solvent perhaps than I'd remembered, and as aggressively orangey. I passed the bottle to Suresh and immediately felt possessive, as though he might not give me my fair share. Relax, I told myself. You're just drinking to keep him company.

He lifted the bottle. Good to see you.

It's good to see you too, I said. I looked at the lights on our left, an occasional car passing, and heard the big road, out of sight, the sounds of a night-time field, crickets and other insects, the trilling of a small bird, the grass breathing. The air was soft and cool on my skin. Suresh gave a big sigh and a small burp.

Eh, I said. This sighing. I've started with that too. What is it?

He shook his head. I don't know, he said, and chuckled.

What have we become, I said. The bottle was in my hand now. I took a much less cautious draught, coughed, and laughed. I wiped my face and handed back the bottle. I didn't think we'd be like this, I said. I thought we'd be more, something.

He laughed. More what?

I don't know. We had all those games. Explorers. Do you remember?

I remember, he said. I looked at his small, slightly plump hands, with their tapering fingers, and felt endeared to him in the old, possessive, dismissive way. I wanted to push him for no reason, but also put my arm around him and protect him from the world.

The bottle returned. I drank. I thought, I said, that we'd go into the world when we were older, do things.

Suresh looked ahead, thought. Why did we have to go out? It's all one world. We were right there in it.

But it didn't feel like that. We were protected, shut away.

We were children, he said. He accepted the return of the bottle. It was now half full. I looked at it a little sadly. I was nicely warm inside.

There's another bottle, he said.

Oh no, I said. I won't drink so much. This is just catching up.

Yes, catching up.

So what's happening with you? I said.

He looked at the palm of his left hand. I don't know, he said. Health's not so good. My son's doing well, though, and my daughter got married two years ago.

But you weren't here for a while?

My son moved away. But then they wanted to come back. They've rebuilt the house, they already have three children.

Mm, I said. And you're working? Or no need?

There's no need, Suresh said. Anyway, I doubt I could now. Look at this. He held out his hand, which seemed to be doing a shaky dance all on its own.

What happened? I said.

He smiled a ruined, rueful little smile. After my wife died, he said, I started drinking more often.

You missed her?

We didn't get along, he said. So you'd think – but somehow it was depressing. I'd become used to resisting her, or trying to stay happy despite her, something like that. When she was gone …

A car horn somewhere.

I drained the santra. The other bottle, I reminded him.

Yes. He passed it to me and this time it was I who cracked the seal, a happy, decisive little sound.

When she was born, I said. Sorry. Gone. When she was gone.

I felt excited, and highly lucid. We were about to get to the nub of the matter. I would solve his problem, and then move on to mine, and we would work it out together. Disciplined thought was what had been lacking but now the moment had arisen.

I don't know, Arun, he said, disappointing me. Things got away from me for a while.

After her death?

He nodded. I felt old. There was no need to work any more. I did for a while. You know how it is. You've spent so long learning a skill.

Yes, I said eagerly. Recently because I've been unwell I haven't been able to work and I feel hollow. I thought I hated it but I discovered that without it I'm lost. I –

He ignored me. But a hand tapped my shoulder.

Eh?

The bottle.

I passed it over.

I still think about those days, you know, I said. For example, the well, the one we used to go to.

What well? said a voice in the darkness.

The well, you must remember, I said. You know, the one near the Narsoba mandir.

Mandir? We never went to Narsobawadi.

Not Narsobawadi. The field temple. You know where I mean.

Well?

Yes, I said. The well.

About a minute later, something very tedious was happening.

Baba, a voice was saying, not exactly patiently but clearly and repeatedly. Baba. We need to go. Wake up, get up.

What? I said. Deepak and a young man I didn't immediately know were there.

Can you look after him? Deepak said. Suresh was standing, but nearly falling down, his face foolish and friendly. He always makes an ass of himself, I thought. I stood, and collapsed like a broken chair.

Here, Deepak said. Put your arm here. Okay. Are you ready? We need to go back now.

Just catching up, I said. Old friends. Childhood.

We didn't know where you were, he said. We've been looking for you for an hour.

*

It's on this road?

It's just up this way, I said. It's not far. But I was wheezing. Oh, I groaned.

You're sure you want to go? Deepak said.

Yes yes, I said. I just want to take a look at the place. You don't have to come, I said. I very much wanted him to come.

To my relief he ignored what I'd said. That's the nice thing about Deepak. He understands how you feel. And yet again, he'd been there when I'd had a shameful moment.

We carried on walking, he slowly in sympathy with his ancient father, and I with effort, but also pleasure. It wasn't yet warm. I had clean clothes on and I'd bathed. Strangely, I'd woken feeling good, and lighter, if a little acid. I supposed we had napped there for some time, Suresh and I. Suresh had been taken home last night, and I didn't remember much else of what had happened.

The rest of the party went off fine? I said.

Deepak gave me a look. Mm, yes, he said.

And now, see the sign? I said. Someone had put up a hand-painted placard: Narsoba mandir.

This is the lane?

This is it.

We turned and walked between waving fields of green wheat. At the end of the lane, a small temple under a tree. This is it? Deepak said.

No no, I said. I don't know what this is. All this, I waved my hand at the small cement structure under the banyan, this is new. Further. Here. I waved my right arm like a signalman and set off ahead, invigorated.

The country opened out, and my mind too expanded, loosened.

See how the sky is here, I said. It was like this even when I was a boy. Deepak was following me and I led till we got to the cucumber field. Still the same smell, green and wet. They still grow cucumbers here, I said. The house in front had been rebuilt, a little bigger and whiter. We walked across the field and a man stopped us.

Are you looking for something?

We're going to the Narsoba mandir, I told him. He stood aside and waved behind him. There it was, a small pukka structure now, painted cream and red with a lion in plaster atop the roof, and an orange flag.

When was all this built? I asked.

He spoke a different Marathi, perhaps inflected with Kannada. Ten years ago, he said.

I used to come here as a child, I said, and he nodded, face blank. The local community leaders collected the money and made it pukka, he said. You can see the names outside.

Don't you want to go in? Deepak asked me.

I'll just take a look, I said. But I felt strange. This new, white structure. We crossed the field of cucumbers, and I removed my shoes and went up the small steps. There was a clean white parapet all around the shrine. But inside it looked familiar. I reached up my hand almost without thinking, and rang the bell. Within, the same stone faces: one in the centre, dark, with a beard etched on. And the two women on either side. I saluted him. Perhaps I even prayed.

There was a sound – a motor, and an automated glugging. I looked out from the balcony and saw a borewell. Near the house, the tank and a young woman in a wrapper washing cucumbers.

You're done? Deepak asked.

I looked behind the temple. An electricity pole leaned like a falling cross into a field of banana trees. And amid a sea of sugar cane, a single gulmohar.

Then I saw the ruined house, behind the tree.

There, I said. I just want to go and look at ...

I came down the steps and set off. A breeze was blowing. I shivered. I should have brought a shawl, I said. Winter's starting.

It'll get cold after Diwali, Deepak said.

Yes.

Why did they have the wedding now?

Something in his family. His brother's moving, so they wanted someone at home.

We passed the woman at the tank, and she looked up.

Deepak greeted her. She smiled at us. Behind her house, a path led out to the ruin. But the forest had retreated. Now it was an island.

What is it, this way?

A place we used to play as children, I said.

Silent, faithful, he walked beside me, and didn't point out that we should return for breakfast, so we could get ready to leave.

We turned off the track, and there it was: the ruin, and, in front of it, the well. As we neared, pigeons flew up from inside.

Has someone cleaned it up? I wondered.

Cleaned what?

This well. It used to be old and blocked, dirty …

We reached it, and looked down. Yes, it was clean. There was a little ornamental ledge inside that I'd forgotten. It looked like a balcony on a haveli. Out of it a young peepal tree was growing, and the pigeons perched there. Below, small birds sang happily. The water smelled fresh.

It looks in use, Deepak said.

Yes.

Do you want to sit for a minute?

Yes, I said. We sat on the remains of the old wall, looking across the fields. I saw the temple's flag.

You found me yesterday, I said. But I'm not drinking again, I want you to know that.

My son's reasonable, mild face.

You were the one, I began. The last time, before I stopped. I'd never discussed it with him. That time I was sick at home, I said.

He said nothing. I heard the dry, rhythmic sound of grasshoppers, then a songbird, wind in the fronds of a coconut palm.

It was after I'd been drinking for months with Borkar and Satpute, after Ratna had left. I'd begun to feel it was time to take control. I experimented with not drinking for a while. And then, certain that it was in fact fine, and there was no problem to speak of, one evening I went drinking homebrew with them, talked God knows what rubbish – I try not to think what, if anything, I told them – bought another bottle of haathbhatti, came home, and finished it. It was still early. She looked at me and went out. Deepak was home studying. I put on the radio, made a lot of noise, talked to myself, sat down with the newspaper, and began to be sick in the corner.

The odd thing is that while I was being sick, which went on intermittently for a long time, I was aware of myself. Not exactly of what was going on. For instance, I had no thought of getting up to go outside. Yet I kept bending down and continuing neatly to vomit quantities of acidic water in the corner. After it began Deepak was sitting next to me with a bucket, wiping my mouth clean. You're fine, he kept saying. You're fine. You're all right. Of course I am, I said once or twice, rather haughtily. What was his problem? You carry on,

I added, continuing to leak. I hadn't eaten – probably that's where things had taken a turn for the worse.

After some time, I'm not sure how long, but I remember being surprised at the voice on the radio and what it said the time was, I had finished. Without further ceremony, I went to sleep. The next day, at first I felt things had gone off rather well. Yes, I'd drunk a little too much. But I was absolutely fine. But a creeping sense of shame began to overtake me, and by the afternoon, as I carried on working, only half aware of what was happening, I began to remember, with hot surges of horror, things I might or might not have said to Borkar and Satpute near the old godown – about Ratna, among other subjects.

Deepak went to school that day, and behaved normally in the evening. To repay him for his care I was particularly ill-tempered and gruff. My wife ignored me. I pretended not to notice. Rather than remembering the things I had said, I remembered my friends' faces, amused and distorted by drinking, shouting, and boasting. How much had I given away? What was the point of keeping it a secret, all that time, sad and reduced by it, only to spurt it out?

During the next few days the episode faded, but I no longer wanted to meet the person who came out when I'd been drinking. A year later, Deepak went away to study in Pune, and then to work. He found his wife, my daughter-in-law. They were training at the same hotel.

You know, I said, looking out at the fields of sugar

cane, the year before you went to Pune. The last time I was drunk.

The sun was hazing over the fields, and it was starting to become warmer. But the year was changing; there had been a chill in the morning, no question about it.

You looked after me, I said. I was – I was sick in the corner of the room.

I heard the sound of the well, its old pump, the busy water.

The last time, I said, before I stopped drinking. Before you went to Pune.

I don't remember, Deepak said.

Yes you do. That time I was sick.

He shook his head. No, he said. I don't remember this at all.

Again I heard the pump, saw, oh, a yellow butterfly, and heard in the background the well, busy, clean. A songbird punctuated the voice of the water with a trill. Ahead, a flash of impossible blue. A kingfisher had flown to an electric wire. It folded its splendour.

The moment unfurled, like pages in an open book.

11

The voice of heaven

A few days later, after we'd been home for a while, when we were having lunch, I said to her, We should have had a daughter.

She looked at me. We had never discussed my escapade with Suresh on the evening of the wedding. When Deepak is there he cushions me from his mother, and his mother from me. Or maybe she just didn't care. The whole wedding had passed off chaotically. The bridegroom's father liked a drink, it turned out, and some of his family had had to take him away and put him to bed when he was trying to dance with one of the neighbours' daughters.

Deepak told me all this on our way home from the Narsoba mandir. So the party became interesting just as I left, I said. He smiled, then laughed.

My wife now smiled slightly. This is where Deepak gets it

from, the ability to remain light-hearted. Though in him it is real amusement. In her, something more like irony. Yes, she said, We should have had a daughter.

It's not such an outlandish thing to say, I said.

No no.

There would have been someone … I said. I thought, someone who always loved me.

She smiled. Yes, she said, we should have had a daughter.

I said, You always –

I always what?

You always just agree. But it isn't really that you agree. You just say something and underneath – I said. I shoved away my plate. I need – I said.

Silence. Outside the door I heard a bird singing loudly.

I need affection, I said. I felt terribly stupid, then angry. I need to talk to someone. This –

You're unhappy with me? But she wasn't worried. She was just getting things clear.

I don't know, I said. Perhaps I'm being a fool. If only someone would comfort me, I thought. I said, I know I haven't been the perfect husband.

She got up to take away the plates. I don't think about it, she said.

But I always feel you want me to be better, I said.

What do you mean?

That you expect more from me, I said. Again, I felt idiotic.

She looked at me. I just think sometimes you make too much work for yourself, she said, being the way you are.

When I came in she said, Look who's come to see you.

Arre, I said. Standing there, diffident and friendly as ever, it was the young malik.

He brightened. He's been coming here since he was a teenager. Now he's not a boy, but a married man, a father of two, and it's he who looks after most of the business.

You've eaten? he said. I'm not disturbing you?

Have you eaten?

I just came from home. I thought I'll come and see you for some time on my way to the shop.

Their house isn't so far from ours, on the main road. A much bigger house, of course. The old man built it, and they all live there.

Have some tea, I said.

No, nothing, he said.

No, this time have some tea, I said.

She went to make it.

Do you need to sit down? he asked. Rest?

I've been resting too much, I said. I'm bored. I miss work. As I said it I realised it was true. I don't remember ever not working for this long. I think I'm ready to start again, I added.

The young malik sat on the floor with me. I sat in my place, despite not working. My right foot found its way to the anvil stone, and pushed against it, reassured by the old resistance.

She came in with the tea. The young malik gave her a big smile and stood to take the cup. He used to come and spend time with us much earlier, when he was learning the trade. His father taught him the basics, but then he came to watch me, also, I think because we accepted him as he was, never expected anything from him.

How are the children? I asked.

He beamed. Avantika is going to learn Chinese in school, he said.

Chinese! I said.

He laughed. It's the language of the future, he said. She knows how to say her name, to say she's an Indian.

That'll be useful, I said, in the future.

He laughed. She can do business in China.

Maybe in the future we'll all be speaking Chinese, I said. Not me, of course, I'll be dead. But you, and everyone else.

I don't know if there'll be chappals in the future, our chappals.

No one will need them, I said. Maybe the indoor chappals. Every surface will be smooth and clean.

He laughed again. Air-conditioned, he said.

Air-conditioned, I said. His children's school, which they go to in a bus every morning, is air-conditioned, a big white building on the road out of town, a more fancy version of Rohan and Sohan's school in Pune.

He dropped his head, looked at his feet. His hair is always neatly stuck down and combed behind his ears, which stick out – lucky ears, Ganpati ears.

I wonder, he said, how long things can go on this way. This trade. After you're gone, you and the other seniors, I'll get machines. There'll be no more of this, making by hand.

He often talks about it.

I can't imagine it, I said. But then I didn't imagine the life my grandchildren lead. My father used to do this work. I gestured at the anvil stone. And my grandfather, how many generations, who knows.

When it's gone, he said, it'll just be gone, it'll be as though it never had been there.

He finished the tea and picked up the cup, stood to take it to the kitchen. You look better than I thought, he said.

I want to work, I said in the evening. Nothing's any good without it.

Yes, she said. You'll be better when there's work again.

I said, What I said earlier – I'm ill.

She was changing into the gown she sleeps in.

I didn't mean it, I said. I sat on the end of the bed.

No? she said. She smiled.

Well, I said. I mean – Oh. Why do you always do this?

Do what?

She lay down next to me. Is there any point in going into it all now? she said.

I don't know, I said. Maybe not.

I know, she said. You like to talk.

I fell asleep, and it was only a moment later, when it was starting to be light and I heard the stove, and water boiling, that I realised it was morning and I hadn't woken during the night.

Two days before Diwali, I came down with a cold. The afternoons smelled of woodsmoke now; in the morning, the air had a bite. I was tired all the time. In the evening, instead of taking my walk, I found myself sitting on the end of the bed. I'll just lie down for a minute, I said. I fell asleep and woke before dawn with a dry mouth.

I didn't work much that day. Preparations were going on for Diwali. She made karanji, chivda, and chakli. I worked for some time, then slept, then worked. I finished a pair. But I felt disconnected. I was so tired.

One is always going to die, from the moment of having been born, but at certain occasions it seems more imminent. I see you coming and going, said the old man, a messenger from the future.

The next night, with the noise and the crackers, I slept badly. I woke shivering and fragile. It was the hinge between one year and the next. What would another twelve months bring? Even the idea was exhausting. Was it the acceptance of my death, at some time in the future, not as an abstract idea but a fact, an illness, a loss of control, then death itself, that made me feel like this? Or something else – the loss of the man I might have been, the man I had always reserved the possibility of becoming?

She cried out from the other room, a cry I hadn't heard in a long time.

What is it? I shouted. I sat up and she rushed in. There was something in her arms, something whitish and dirty.

Look! she said and then bending to the bundle, You're back! He's back.

I see that, I said. I went to her and took the cat from her. He settled down, resting his front paws on my shoulder as usual.

So you came back? I said. Green eyes looked wearily into mine. He yowled.

Get him some food, for God's sake, I said. And what happened to you? I asked. You're filthy. Are you hurt?

But when I put him down there didn't seem to be any wounds. He was tired and bedraggled. She gave him milk and bhakri, then a fish head, and he ate it and began to wash himself.

He came back, she said. I knew he would. Her eyes shone.

I didn't know, I said. I thought …

I knew, she said.

I patted her shoulder. I'm tired, I said. I didn't get enough rest at night. I'll sleep until lunch. But I put on the radio, quietly, so that I wouldn't feel alone.

As soon as I got on the bed and arranged the blanket, I looked down to see green eyes examining me. He hesitated, then jumped lightly up, and stretched out next to my stomach. At once, he began to rumble; I felt the vibrations and his warmth at my abdomen, and relaxed, as though someone else had taken over responsibility for my existence.

It was no longer really morning, but not yet time for lunch. She was busy in the kitchen. I heard neighbours' voices, car horns outside, the different traffic of a holiday, and film music. The clay lamp burned on the doorstep, and the rangoli was neat and pretty just outside, white and green and red patterns of chalk, slightly shaky here and there, though she does it well; its naivety and impermanence make it more beautiful.

It was Diwali, and every good thing was at hand. My wife was in the next room. There was food in the house. Later, we'd see my grandson. The long ago past, my parents, Suresh, the parijatak bush, the Narsoba temple in the cucumber field, the well, the house where I'd grown up, all were distant, like a fever dream. Yesterday's fears and pain seemed like a story in the newspaper. And, for once, restlessness and the urge to move towards the next thing were quiet.

This is the Voice of Heaven, said the radio, and next in our special music programme of devotional songs we are playing you an early recording by Pandit Bhimsen Joshi.

The old bullfrog.

But the familiar tabla beats began, and the background incantation: Vitthala Vitthala Vitthala Vitthala …

Aa-aaa-aa-aa-aaaaa!

The voice was young, not the stentorian tones I remembered. It leapt for joy.

Prrrr, prrrr, prrr, prrr.

I couldn't remember my anxieties, my hopes, my plans, my fears. I was carried away, and there was nothing to do but let go. The rhythm and warmth of the world flowed through me and like a lover I opened myself, and marvelled at my luck.

Acknowledgements

I'd like to thank:

In Kolhapur, Mr Vinayak Kadam of
Adarsh Charmodyog Centre, and Irfan Inamdar.

Salil Bijur, Dr Arti Khatter and Dr Farrokh Wadia.

In Norwich, Jason Larke and all at Van Dal Shoes.

A chapter of this novel first appeared in *Granta: India*
in January 2015. Thanks to Ian Jack and Yuka Igarashi.

Lettice Franklin and all at Fourth Estate in London;
V. K. Karthika and all at HarperCollins in Delhi.

The trustees and judges of the Desmond Elliott
Prize and the Betty Trask Prize.